Copyright © 2014 Torey Irving

ISBN:0692218831
ISBN-13:978-0692218339
Passion Ink Publishing

DESIGN OF THEIR HEARTS

Dedication

I dedicate this book to those that have been abused, sexually, mentally and spiritually by anyone. What I want you to get from this book is that Love is still out there for you.

ACKNOWLEDGMENTS

First of all, I would like to thank my Lord and Savior. Jesus Christ. Without Him, my talents and my drive to reach my goals wouldn't exist.

I also would like to thank my parents. I was lucky enough to be blessed with a mom and dad in my life and they are my role models. I hope that when they read my work, they would proud of me.

I like to say thanks to everyone from my brother and sister and friends that support what I do. Your support is so appreciated and I hope that you enjoy my work. Thank you. Thank you Jae Elle for all of your continued support. Also, thank you for editing my book. You are appreciated to no end and I can't tell you enough. Thank you for everything.

Last, but not least. I like to say a special thanks to my beautiful wife, Shelba Irving. Thank you for your support and understanding throughout the process of putting this book together. I couldn't have asked for a better wife. Thanks for your encouraging words and constant pushing me. I definitely needed it. I hope when you read this book, you feel a major part of yourself in it. Because without your love, I wouldn't have been able to put as much love as I did into this book. I love you baby! To Londyn and Anaya, Daddy loves you and thank you both for your love. My blessings.

Thank you all!!!

Praying a soul mate into existence.

I pray that you come and find me because I am ready to be found. If our God has it fit for me to find you, then I pray that you make yourself available to be found. I promise to never hurt you and I promise to never forsake you. I promise that I will love you if you allow me to find you. I kneel before you Lord and pray that the love of my life is out there somewhere doing the same. I hope they are kneeling before you asking for me as I am doing right now. I pray that the person you have designed for me has a kind and gentle heart, but loves me strong enough to tell me when I am wrong. I pray that the heart you have created to match mines will be caring, loving and persistent enough to keep looking for me when I am lost. I pray that you continue to mold me into the person I want to be for you and for the person you see fit to love me. I pray...I pray...I pray you my love into existence. In God's name, I pray. Amen!

CHAPTER 1

The nights were beginning to get more and more different for Deron Jamison, the 12 year old antisocial son of Paul and Gloria Jamison. He was a shy and sometimes nervous only child that longed for other siblings. The older he got and the more things changed around him, the happier he was that he was the only child. Deron stood about 5'5 and weighed 90 pounds soaking wet, but he carried the attitude of a 6'6 230 pound linebacker. Staying where he stayed, he had to possess that kind of attitude.

Paul Jamison was a calm natured family man and successful car salesman. He stood a tall and muscular built man and all of the ladies that came to his car lot loved to see and talk to the cool smooth talker. He had a light caramel complexion and veins ripped through his skin making the older men in his office envious of him. Also, making the women secretly wish he was single.

The 6'4 220 pound man with hazel eyes who always seemed to wear a smile knew the affect he had on the people around him, but he made sure to keep God and his family first. He kept pictures of Gloria and Deron everywhere in his office, to serve as a reminder to everyone that entered his area; he was a happily married man.

Gloria was an elementary school teacher and she loved taking care of her family. Deron's favorite TV show was the Cosby show and he and Paul loved having their own personal Claire Huxtable. She would awake before they did to make sure they woke to the smell of breakfast and coffee.

She was a petite, dark skinned woman with short naturally curly hair and she had the type of figure other women were jealous of. She stood a tiny 5'2 and weighed a lusty 130 pounds. Gloria was also admired where she worked and just like Paul, everyone knew she was happily married, but of course, the men still hit on Gloria and Paul didn't like it one bit. It was one of the very few things that upset him the most.

The Jamison's were the perfect family to everyone they stayed around, worked with and went to church with. They stayed in a shoddy part of Dallas and because of that, they became a little overprotective of Deron. What people didn't know about the Jamison's was that over the past few years, things hadn't been what they appeared.

Paul lost his job about 2 years ago and had been working odd jobs just to make ends meet and Gloria was no longer teaching due to lay-offs in the Dallas Independent School District. Lately, Deron noticed that his once muscular dad had started drinking and arguing with Gloria more and more. No longer the cool and calm dad, he was now angry all of the time and was rarely seen without a bottle in his hand.

Gloria had finally succumbed to of all of the advances from the men at her job and one in particular, Mr. Jacobs, introduced her to the barbarous world of drugs and adultery. Once Paul, the new Paul, found out about Gloria's affairs, he became abusive to not only Gloria, but also Deron. The alcoholic and abusive Paul had been around for the last year and it turned the quiet, antisocial Deron, into even more of an outsider. Gloria had become the neighborhood crack head and her once desirable body had deteriorated miserably, to the point where her body was now frail and lacked anything that would bring about sexual fantasies from the men that once desired her.

CHAPTER 2
1988 DERON, 12 YEARS OLD

Deron had awakened from his struggled sleep and it wasn't the loud train that exploded through the projects of Oak Cliff, a small town inside of Dallas, TX. He heard his dad beating his mom senseless and if he didn't want to be part of that party, then he best stay put right there in the safeness of his room. Paul would always tell Deron "You step to me like a man son, and I'm gon' beat you down like a man, boy." He was only 12 years old, but he'd seen more tears come from his mom than laughs.

Miss Velma, the neighbor and sometimes the person that would watch over Deron, would call the police, but Paul played them living in the projects to his advantage. It took the cops so long to come that Paul would convince Gloria that him beating her was somehow her fault and she would tell the cops nothing was going on. Miss Velma always threatened Deron saying, "Boy if I ever finds out you ended up like yo' alcoholic daddy, I will hunt you down and kill you." as she dabbed the corners of her mouth after every sentence.

Deron really didn't understand much about what an alcoholic was, but he was smart enough to know that if someone threatened to kill him for being one, then it must be something horrible. Miss Velma was a 63 year old woman that watched, or babysat, all of the kids in the neighborhood. She had a head full of shiny, gray hair and she would always wear the same blue and green overcoat. The kids talked about her, but had too much respect for the strong and strict older lady to disrespect her to her face.

Miss Velma had the kind of keen voice that scared the younger kids and the voice that the older kids, like Deron, had to respect. He often wondered how an old lady that struggled to walk, had trouble seeing, and seemed to be in pain every time he would see her, possessed so much power.

Deron walked closer and closer to his door. All of the banging and screams were starting to scare him. Opening it slightly, he saw his dad's sweaty forearms and fist going upside Gloria's face repeatedly as she tried in vain to stop him. Paul stood tall and stout, so her efforts were pointless.

"Boy, you wanna be a man tonight huh?" Paul asked while Deron stood in the doorway of his room.

"Baby.....baby go back to your room, momma is ok." Gloria cried out while holding her hands up to her battered face. Her eyes were swollen and her cheeks looked as if they had been stoned.

"Yea boy, listen to your crackhead momma and go back in the room before you be next."

Deron saw his mother's tears blending in with the sweat on her face and her hair was drenched in her own blood. She looked at him and tried her best to crack a smile, but all of the running blood told her she was a damn fool for trying. It amazed Deron how Gloria could lie right to his face and tell him she was ok when he could plainly tell she wasn't. Call it trying to be strong or call it saying what Paul wanted her to

say, but Deron knew the truth. He listened to both and went
back in his room, closed the door and cried himself to sleep.

Deron wasn't like normal kids his age. His momma was
a crackhead and it embarrassed him. He was embarrassed
because he knew what a crackhead was before he knew the
meaning of an alcoholic, but in all fairness, Paul was the one
who explained what a crackhead was and why Gloria is one.
Paul was an alcoholic and from what Deron knew, an
alcoholic was someone who screams and beats people crazy,
but he was sure there was more to it.

The quiet and solemn pre teen couldn't remember the
last time he got a hug and kiss from Gloria or the last time he
watched the Dallas Cowboys game with his dad. It was once
a normal thing in the Jamison's household and it's something
Deron came to really miss more than anything. He would
hear the kids at school talking about it and it seemed like a
cool thing to do. All holidays were spent at Miss Velma's
house and she always had a house full of kids, so he never
really got the attention he always craved and because of that,
the easily angered Deron got into plenty of fights. He would
always tell Gloria that he loved her and her response lately
was always "that's so sweet baby." or "me too baby." He no
longer actually heard the words directed towards him and he
was never taken seriously. Anytime Deron ever had anything
to say, he was always interrupted by something, so he learned
to say little and if he did have a lot to say, hurry up and get it
out.

Paul was done beating on Gloria and while Deron stood
there looking through the small crack in the door from which
he opened. He saw Paul smoking a cigarette and drinking
some of his grown people juice. So he snuck out of his room
in search of his mother, but she was nowhere to be found
until he heard her cries in the bathroom. She just stood
there, watching herself in the mirror crying. Her face was
painted with bruises and scratches. She wore her own blood,

and her hair was pounded with sweat. The more Gloria stared at herself, the more tears ran down her battered face. Deron stood there watching Gloria clean herself up and he started to speak, but she beat him to it.

"Tomorrow is a big day for you baby, are you ready for it?"

"Yes momma, I can't wait." Deron said with a counterfeit tone.

"It's the first day of school and you're going to be in the 7th grade. My baby in Junior High! I'm so excited honey! Go get in the bed baby and I will be in there soon to tuck you in." Gloria said while running a face towel down her discolored face.

"Yes ma'am." Deron said as he walked away with his head hanging low. His eyes drooped as he slowly sauntered down the hallway which held family portraits of what seemed like a different family.

Gloria was right, tomorrow was the first day of school, but it was also Deron's birthday. He didn't bother reminding Gloria because he had finally come to terms that this is his life now. He could pout, bitch and moan, or accept it for what it was. His life was no longer the same and it now consisted of let downs, financial problems and being borderline poor. His family was no longer the perfect family that everyone wanted and Deron understood that more than anyone. He figured his dad beat Gloria so much that he couldn't find it to be her fault that her memory was now fading helplessly into a blind abyss.

"Say little nigga, get yo' ass in the goddamn bed fo' yo' ass get beat next." Paul yelled and coughed into the hallway, causing Deron to dash hurriedly back to his room. He quickly jumped into his bed and threw the covers over his head praying his dad wouldn't come in. Most times Deron would pull out a compilation of old poetry that consisted of his favorite poet, Walt Whitman.

The girls often wondered why he spoke the way that he did, with such conviction and passion and most of them thought he was weird, but not the one that mattered most, Janiya Brakens. She was the one girl that Deron felt differently about. Something was special about this girl and he knew it.

Once he started thinking about her, the covers erased from his face and a smile emerged, leaving him in a world where no one existed but he and the "dazzling Janiya" One of the many names he had for her.

They both had gone to R. S. Stevens Elementary School and Deron was determined to make her notice him since they hadn't spoken one word to each other or even intentionally locked eyes. Janiya was a brown skin goddess in the eyes of Deron. She had long wavy hair and was built similar to the way his mom use to be, a small petite frame that all of the boys liked. Deron thought about Janiya often and it made him wonder about love and the possibilities.

There Deron sat in a still moment's time, wondering, pondering on the evolution of the possibility that he will, that he could ever love Janiya the way waves love the ripples in its' oceans, or the way clouds love to form images of beauty in God's sky. Deron thought about how he would run to Janiya, as he heard her heartbeat calling out to him like a baby bird calling for his momma. As he lay in his bed, he saw Janiya smiling at him as only she could.

Only she could make his heart cry out in endless joy. In that very moment, Deron saw love. Once the thought of Janiya had come and gone, Deron laid there and prayed like Miss Velma taught him. He prayed that God would one day show him that there's more to life than what he was seeing. He also prayed for Gloria and Paul, but he believed if they knew that he even prayed at all, they wouldn't want him to do it.

Deron tried to fall asleep, but the sounds he heard kept him awake. Gloria and Paul were yelling at each other, so Deron thought. Gloria was screaming loudly, but these were different screams. He didn't hear much from Paul, but he did hear words that a kid his age shouldn't hear. Maybe Paul was too drunk and Gloria was too high to remember how much hatred they had for each other. They were enjoying the pleasures of sex. Latarion, another kid that stayed at Miss Velma's house, schooled Deron early on what sex was and he said his dad would let him watch porno's with him. Deron just kept his head under the covers and forced himself to fall asleep.

Morning had finally come and Deron was getting ready for school while Gloria and Paul were still asleep. He always wondered if other 12 year olds had to get up on their own and get up on time. His favorite TV show was the Cosby Show and he started wishing that he was a part of a family like that. A family that was together, they had fun and most of all, they were happy. That's how his family use to be before Paul lost his job and became an alcoholic and before Gloria lost her job, had affairs, and became a crackhead. The Cosby Show was the life to Deron and anytime he had the chance to watch that show, he would jump at it. It somehow made him get away from his reality.

"Dad? Dad wake up." Deron whispered.

"What you want lil fucker" Paul spoke back with his raspy voice.

"I need a ride to school."

"Get yo crackhead momma to take you, shit. You know where the school is, better yet, walk!"

Deron walked to school plenty of times before so that wasn't a problem, but he just hated walking to school because they stayed in a bad part of Dallas. On the days he had to walk to school, Deron saw gangs, drugs, and prostitutes, but he kept his head down and stayed on his trail to his destination.

The morning was nice and hot with a few clouds filling the sky and Deron liked being able to look up and see the sun shining while the rays pierced through the crisp white clouds. He also loved seeing the shapes of the clouds. He would pretend to see a puppy, a rabbit and sometimes he would even see the eye-catching Janiya up in the clouds. He walked along the sidewalk that was crowded with students waiting to enter the school for the first time. The same soiled British Knights tennis shoes that he wore last year pasted themselves to his feet and the blue jeans Deron wore tried desperately to reach his ankles, but came up a few inches short.

His shirt had a hole in it, but he managed to hide it by tucking it in to his pants. However, Deron looked up and smiled because of who he saw getting dropped off. All of the clouds ceased from existing, the chatter from kids was erased and the chirping of birds suddenly came to an end. The hairs erected themselves from Deron's arms as time seemed to slow down while an accepting tingle crept into Deron's heart and made itself comfortable. He had seen the alluring Janiya plenty of times, but never got this feeling. Poetic thoughts filled his brain as he gazed at something, someone so unbelievably captivating.

If you could count all smiles that have been smiled and see all the love that has been cherished, you would have a small sample of what Deron felt for the beautiful Janiya. If you've seen all the flowers in the world, or witnessed each undulation of wave in an endless ocean, then you would have seen how Deron wanted his love for Janiya to blossom effortlessly in the gardens of her heart.

If you have ever seen love in the eyes of a man for his lady, then you would see but a mere fraction of the love Deron desired to have for Janiya. His love for her could be seen in his eyes, felt in his touch, heard loudly through his voice, and it even boisterous in Deron's whispers and prayers.

After gazing blissfully, Deron thought about speaking, but he couldn't bring himself to act out what his mind told him he wanted. Her name was Janiya Brakens and she was a princess in the young eyes of Deron. He considered her the most stunning person he's ever been around, including his mom, before all the drugs and beatings handed down by Paul.

Janiya was a very light complexion and beauty rained down her like the ocean spilling down a waterfall. Her hair was dark as the midnight sky and long with silky waves cascading down her back. Her eyes wore an astonishing hazel hue and twinkled and shined like the moon over the night's lake.

"Boy you might as well stop looking at her, she don't want no poor ghetto boy like you." Said Jasmine Stephens, the bully that Deron prayed would end up at another school. He didn't bother saying anything back to Jasmine because she was a big girl that hit like a grown man. Deron finally tore himself from watching Janiya so she wouldn't be creeped out.

He was sure he was in love every single time he caught himself watching Janiya…in love with the idea of loving Janiya. He understood that people and kids his age thought he was weird for thinking the way he does. When Deron was younger, his mom always told him "Son you have an old soul, but it's ok to be that way, your father was the same way." Maybe Deron was in love because of what she symbolized to him. Happy, rich, important, beautiful, and most of all, wanted.

He believed he loved Janiya by simply watching her because she made him believe that there was something more to life than what he had at home. He had something to look forward to other than being yelled at daily for something he didn't do, or watching his dad beat the crap out of his mom.

13

Deron was able to dream of a life without seeing Paul passed out drunk and Gloria overdosed on drugs. This was why he would always watch Janiya. She was his blue sky, his vacation on the beach and his Cosby show.

Deron would always watch her as she tried her best to fit in with the regular kids. Janiya seemed to be your normal rich kid who tried their best to downplay that she's rich and had everything she could ever want.

From their old days in elementary school, Deron never saw Janiya wear the same clothes twice to school, but he on the other hand, would sometimes wear the same clothes, in the same week. Being only twelve years old, with today being Deron's birthday, he had a lot of responsibility. Taking care of his abused, beaten, crack head mom, and somehow making sure Paul didn't kill her when he gets drunk.

He had to basically fend for himself and most times it left him questioning his faith, along with everything else. He believed in God, but lately had more and more questions that he asked and had no clue where the answers would come from.

Deron was an undersized ball of explosives; it didn't take much to set him off, but because of his size, he took his share of beatings. They were mostly to protect and defend Janiya in hopes she would one day notice the feeble, yet protective Deron.

It was nothing for him to get into these fights and the pain didn't bother Deron because sadly, he'd become numb to it. Paul was not only beating Gloria senseless, but now abusing Deron to the point he'd walk to school looking like a sad dog that got the bad end of brawl, limping with a battered leg.

Janiya and Deron found themselves in the same recess class and regardless of how the night was for Deron, the first day of school was starting out to be a great day for him. He sat alone at the edge of the old grimy wooden bleachers eating the tuna fish sandwich that he prepared for himself and made sure to keep a close eye on Janiya.

He scowled at all of the other boys that watched her, but he also paid close attention to Janiya. If someone entered Deron in a contest to see how well he knew Janiya, it would be an easy win for him. Her favorite color was a soft purple and her favorite ear rings were some light green studs that I'm guessing were her birthstone.

Janiya loved to sing when she was alone and Deron loved to watch her lips part ways while he imagined the remarkable sounds she produced. He could also tell when Janiya had a lot on her mind and he wanted so badly to go up to her, lay her head on his shoulders the way Claire Huxtable would lie her head on Cliff's and listen to anything she had to release.

Instead, Deron just watched her until recess was over. She headed her way and he headed his. Deron was always the last one to his class because he had to make sure she made it safely to her class.

Jasmine made sure she followed and had some words to say.

"Say lil boy, why you always watching that girl? I told you that nobody don't want you cuz' your family is poor and she is rich. You might as well stick to somebody on your level, besides; I have a better chance of being with her than you do." Jasmine said laughing uncontrollably.

"Jasmine, you don't know what you're talking about, I don't want that girl. I'm only 12 years old, I don't even like that girl." Deron said, lying through his teeth.

"Whatever, you're telling a story and I know it. I see you all the time watching her at recess."

"Why you always gotta be watching me?" Deron snapped, forgetting that he was talking to a bully.

Jasmine was just about to go up side his head, but luckily a teacher walked by and told them to hurry to class. Deron walked away smiling that he didn't get beat down, but he also walked away with Janiya on his mind. He thought to himself if it was possible to be in love with someone that you have never spoken to or physically touched.

How could he know so much about someone and feel as if he didn't even exist in her eyes? He was in love with the simple hint of Janiya even knowing his name. He promised himself that from that moment, that instant, he would live to protect Janiya. He would live to see a smile painted upon her angelic face. Deron wanted all of her pain, all of her hurt, all of her worries to somehow be taken away from her and given to him. He had nothing at home to live for, so why not live for the girl he loved and make sure she's at least happy.

CHAPTER 3
JULY 20, 1988 JANIYA 12 YEARS OLD

"Good morning baby, how did my angel sleep?" Janiya's mother, Edna asked.

Edna was a slender, yet gorgeous and tall woman. She possessed a pair of the most striking dark brown eyes a woman could ask for. Her caramel skin was flawless and it should be, considering how much money her family had. That was gossip around town about the Brakens. They should look perfect because they are rich.

Her hair had no blemishes, it was elongated and coiled to perfection. She walked with the confidence that many other women only dreamed about possessing. She loved her life as a stay at home mom, mostly because people envied what she had.

"Good morning mother, I slept well." Janiya replied while wiping the sleep from her heavy eyes.

"That's good baby. Lorretta made breakfast for you, it's ready at the table." Edna said, while looking down at the local newspaper.

Lorretta was their maid and the nanny. Janiya saw more of her than her own mother and step father. Lorretta normally dropped her off and picked her up from school, dance class, and piano practice. Her parents would normally attend all of Janiya's functions, but Lorretta knew more about how hard she worked and how much she enjoyed dance and piano practice.

"So… baby how is school? Are you making some friends yet?" Edna asked while still buried in the newspaper. Janiya wanted so badly to just grab the paper and rip it to shreds.

"Yes mother, I've made some good friends, but some of the kids still pick on me and call me the rich kid." Janiya said while eating the pancakes that Lorretta prepared for her.

"That's good baby, but don't talk with food in your mouth, ok?" Edna said, basically dismissing the fact that Janiya was getting pick on and getting called out of her name.

"Oooh mother, there is this boy at school that always……"

"Good morning dear, where is my coffee?" Janiya's step father, Phillip Brakens, said while kissing Edna on her begging cheek, interrupting Janiya in the process.

He came rushing in trying to finish tying his tie and didn't realize Janiya was in the middle of a conversation. That was the way the Brakens household worked.

Janiya's biological father died when she was three years old in what her mother calls a fatal car accident. Edna had met Phillip Brakens shortly after that and soon he was Janiya's father.

She didn't like him at all, but Edna forced her to call him father and forced her to act like the perfect daughter. If only Edna knew what Janiya had to deal with, when it came to Phillip.

Phillip use to be a police officer patrolling the streets of Oak Cliff, but now was this big time congressman that made a lot of money doing Lord knows what.

Janiya noticed how much the overpowering Phillip controlled Edna since he was the bread winner in the family. Edna basically got what she wanted as long as she knew who was in charge.

She didn't work, well she does if you considered shopping and hanging out with her girls, work. On the outside, the Brakens looked like the perfect family, but there were a lot of people that just didn't know about their family.

The Brakens was a money-driven family and Janiya didn't like it. Sure, she got all the material things she wanted. She had a nanny that took her where she needed to go, tucked her in at night, and listened to her without interrupting her. Janiya loved the fact she got that from Lorretta, but she would rather have all of that from my parents.

"Janiya baby, Lorretta is ready to drop you off at school." Edna said while fiddling around with her curly hair.

"Mother, why can't you, or father, take me to school? All of the other kids have their parents drop them off." Janiya begged.

"Yes honey, it's because they have no choice. You should feel fortunate that you have choices and that you have the things that you have. I'm sure those kids' parents wouldn't be taking them to school if they had the choice to have someone else do it."

Once again, Edna had missed the point Janiya was trying to make. She began talking about how fortunate Janiya was and how rich they were. Janiya huffed while walking up to her clueless mother. She kissed her on her cheek and stormed out of the house dragging her light purple backpack that Lorretta bought her.

Janiya frowned as she jumped in the back seat. She saw Lorretta looking at her in the rear view mirror. Janiya folded her arms across her chest and gazed outside the window. She was angry and Lorretta knew it. All Janiya wanted, was to be normal like all of the other kids at her school.

She didn't care that they had a huge house with a four car garage and all the land that mother and father dreamed of, so she heard them say. The six cars they owned wasn't a big deal for the simple Janiya.

Lorretta kept watching Janiya huff and puff in the back seat until she finally had heard enough of it.

"Chica, what's wrong with you?" Lorretta asked with her thick accent. Lorretta was an alluring Latino woman and Janiya always wondered why she settled to be her nanny and maid. Her smooth, cloud like skin and perfectly placed cheekbones was admired by Janiya. Lorretta had long silky brown hair and she always wore it back in a ponytail. The way she walked enhanced her curves and made Janiya practice it when she was alone in her room.

Janiya was confused about Lorretta's career choice, but she was pretty sure that Phillip paid her well. Lorretta was just so incredibly exotic to Janiya. She really looked up to her and it didn't make sense to her.

"Nothing." Janiya replied while looking out of the moist window wondering how it felt to be the kids that were walking to school.

"Come on mami, if it was nothing you wouldn't be sulking back there. I know something's wrong, so just tell me."

Janiya continued to ignore Lorretta and kept watching the world go on outside her window.

Lorretta kept trying and Janiya kept ignoring her, but they both knew that she really wanted to talk. Lorretta said the very thing that made Janiya want to speak to her.

"Fine chica, I won't bother asking you about that boy from your school that you were gonna tell your mommy about. I won't ask why you got so excited and I won't ask why you are in my back seat blushing now." Lorretta said with a huge grin on her face that showed exactly how deep her dimples were.

"Ok, ok Lorretta." Janiya said blushing with her head down in embarrassment.

"Now hurry up and spill it mami, we're almost at your school and if your parents ask, tell them I told you that you are twelve years old and you're too young to be thinking about boys." Lorretta replied.

"So there's this cute boy at school that everyone talks about and it makes me kinda sad, but I can't say anything because then I won't be like the normal kids and that's why I like this school, it makes me feel like one of the regular kids. Anyways, he's very quiet and I always find myself watching him, but I don't even think he knows that I exist...."

"Well, what if he did? What if he thought the same about you?" Lorretta said while interrupting Janiya. It was one of the few times she didn't mind being interrupted. For some reason, it was always ok when Lorretta did it. Maybe it was because she wasn't interrupting her to start another conversation with someone else like Phillip did earlier today.

"I don't know what I would do. I probably just keep doing the same thing I'm doing now." Janiya replied while playing around with her fingers nervously. Lorretta and Janiya talked about the boy the rest of the way to school.

Janiya even pointed her quiet crush out to the giggling Lorretta and she also thought he was cute. She drove off with a smile on her face and Janiya stayed there until she disappeared.

Janiya strolled into her classroom and she caught him looking at her for the first time. She sometimes felt his eyes moving over her, but she never locked eyes with him.

Janiya was twelve years old, but there was something about this boy that made her really want to get to know him. She laughed secretly to herself when she realized that she had found her first crush.

Janiya often caught herself singing when she was alone at recess. She always imagined that quiet, hugely underdressed boy hearing her. There was a glow to him and he seemed so different from anyone she had known.

His name was Deron, Deron Jamison and like all girls, she imagined herself having his last name. Janiya Jamison, she would always whisper to herself as she brushed her hair at night before she went to sleep. Janiya always thought she was crazy for doing that. She knew she would just die if Deron ever found out that's what she did. Finally, Janiya made it into her classroom and she sat down in her assigned seat still thinking about Deron.

"What are you thinking about girl?" Janiya's best friend Layla asked. Layla was her only friend that her parents knew about because her family was rich like hers. Their dads would sometimes go play golf together. Layla would come sleep over so they would keep each other company since they were both the only child.

"I'm not thinking about anything Layla." Janiya replied, but her lowered head and constant shifting eyes told Layla that she was lying.

"J, you are a terrible liar." Layla barked. They gave each other nicknames in the attempt to be one of the cool normal kids. Janiya's name was J and she gave Layla, L. It was simple, but it worked for the two young girls.

"Anyway J, are you going to the school dance next Friday?" Layla asked with her eyebrows sprouting up in excitement. She loved to go to school dances and be around all the boys. They all liked Layla and Janiya definitely understood why. She was gorgeous to the young Janiya. She had a light caramel complexion with hazel eyes and her hair was long and curly, like Chili's from the singing group, TLC. Janiya had always thought Layla was the more tantalizing one of the two. In fact, she didn't believe herself to be too eye-catching. She still thought she was in that young girl stage where her body had not even started developing, but all of the other girls around her had started developing last year and Layla was definitely one of the girls.

"No, I don't think I'm going to that dance. If I go, you know I will just end up watching all of the boys fight over you and ignore me like always."

"Come on J, you have to come." Layla begged. Janiya tuned out Layla, the teacher, and the kids that were playing in class. She tuned them out and thought what if Deron was there? What if he showed up and she didn't go? Janiya honestly didn't think he would show up because the word around school about Deron was that his dad is an alcoholic and his mom is a crackhead.

It was also rumored around school that he was borderline homeless. Even knowing all of this about Deron, Janiya was still intrigued by the dangerous, yet calming, stillness of him. She felt that Deron was different than anyone she had known and that was what she liked about him.

He didn't seem like everyone else that knew she was the "rich girl" and gave her whatever she wanted except what she needed. Janiya saw, and felt, that Deron was the one person that not only needed what she needed, but he wanted to give her what she needed more than he wanted to receive it. At least, she hoped that was the case.

"Hello, snap snap." Layla whispered all wide eyed, hoping to grab Janiya's distant attention back. She wanted so badly to tell Layla about Deron, but she was one of the kids that always talked about him. Janiya confessed to her anyway.

"Fine, I'll go to the stupid dance." Janiya shot back at her. Layla sat back in her cold wooden seat thanking Janiya, sarcastically.

"L, why do you always talk about Deron?" Janiya finally brought herself to ask and she knew that she would regret asking Layla that question.

Yes, they were best friends, but she was still a rich girl that craved all of the attention she got. Layla thought she was better than everyone else except Janiya because she knew her family was just as rich as hers. She talked bad about the kids at the school, but tried her best to be like them when she was around them.

"Who is Deron?" Layla asked with a clueless look in her eye.

"You're talking about the poor homeless boy with the crackhead momma?" Layla asked before Janiya could answer her original question. Her eyes were narrowed and her nose was drawn up and wrinkled in disgust. Mr. Johnson, their teacher, coughed, signaling for the talkative girls to be quiet and pay attention.

"He's not homeless." Janiya whispered back while keeping her eyes up ahead at Mr. Johnson

"He's about to be and I know that's not who you were thinking about. J, I know you don't like that boy, all the kids talk about him bad and if people find out you like him, they will talk about you too." Layla whispered back with her guttural sounds. Janiya ignored Layla and couldn't wait for recess to arrive.

She daydreamed about Deron, wondering how it felt to be the one kid that everyone talked about. Janiya's sweaty palms were planted on her cheeks and she stared outside still thinking about Deron. She also wondered how it felt to be borderline homeless, your dad an alcoholic, and your mother a crackhead. It had to be tough to deal with that and how could he possibly notice her when he has all that to worry about.

The recess bell rang and Layla grabbed Janiya's dangling arm, hurrying her outside of the classroom so she could pick up where they left off about Deron.

"Now, did I hear you right? You like Deron?" She asked curiously. Layla's eyes were flaming read and she wore a frown on her face with her hands clutching her hips.

"L, all I asked was why you talked about him." Janiya replied without even looking at Layla. She looked Janiya up and down while smacking her lips.

"I should've known you would end up liking him since he was always getting into fights over you." Layla said as she walked away from her in embarrassment.

"Wait!" Janiya screamed, getting the attention of a number of nosy students around them. Janiya was clueless about Layla's comment. She held on tight to her backpack and ran up to Layla, hoping she would explain herself.

"What are you talking about? He gets into fights over me?" Janiya questioned, while grabbing Layla's arm.

"Yea girl, I thought you knew. Everybody else knew that he liked you and anybody that bothered you; he would always end up fighting them. Seriously Janiya, you can't fall for this boy. You will be the laughing stock of this school and I'm not going to hang with you if they talking about you too. So you have a decision to make." Layla stared at her, waiting on an answer until she finally shook her, head and walked off. Once again, Janiya ran up to Layla, this time it was just to walk with her and at that point, her decision was made.

CHAPTER 4

1990 Deron 14 years old

Two years and some months had passed and Deron still had yet to utter one word to his delightful Janiya. He continued to watch her and still enjoyed the times when she sung to herself, imagining that she was singing to him. She hung around some girl that Deron figured was her best friend; she was beautiful too, but no match when it came to Janiya. She was his best friend and that was hard to say since they hadn't spoken one word to each other or at least made eye contact.

Janiya had a way about her that spoke to Deron without words. It sent his mind wandering about things way beyond his time. Janiya was often times the reason he chose to keep living, as if he was living for that one precious moment to see her, to think about her, to hang around places she'd been.

Just the mere thought of loving this person made Deron see things in a way that was so special. He had no choice but to keep living and keep experiencing it. Understandably, it was his greatest weakness that he loved to encounter. Aside from his love for Janiya, his life at home was more horrible than ever. Deron felt he had to walk on egg shells that were already on egg shells. His dad continued to drink, mom continued to do drugs. The police continued to make frequent stops to their home because of the beatings Gloria took.

Deron created a space in his mind that would free him from his house, and of course Janiya was there. He could only do that for so long. Eventually, he would have to come back to reality and raise himself with a little help from Miss Velma.

He would spend time at Miss Velma's house, but it was no better because the kids there were still better off than he was. Also, they would torment Deron just like the kids at school.

Miss Velma was a nice elderly lady that was very hard on Deron and in a way, he appreciated it. He appreciated things that kids hated, like discipline, being told what to do and chores. It's not much fun to have parents that let you do whatever you want and Miss Velma recognized it.

He had the parents that could not care less if he was there or not. They could not care less that he wore shoes with holes in them, and they could not care less that he didn't have money to eat lunch with. Often sneaking food form leftover lunch trays was a skill he mastered.

This night in particular started off bad, and of course it was getting worse. Deron was in his room and just like clockwork; his dad stumbled in the house, slamming the door behind him.

"Baby, momma wants you to stay in your room ok?" Gloria asked with loads of bags under her eyes.

"Ok." Deron replied, looking up and then back out of his window. He felt his mom still standing there in his doorway, so he turned to her and as he did, a single tear ran down her face.

Her eyes were sunken and her skin was pale. She looked up at Deron and walked in his room and closed the door quietly behind her. He watched his mom as she walked closer to him and he began to feel bad for her, which made him angry. Here was a woman that never once told Deron she loved him, here was a woman that let his father beat on her and for no reason. Here was a woman that was so strung out on drugs that Deron almost weighed more than she did, but he still felt bad for her. Deron had so much anger towards her, but loved her at the same time. He just wanted it all to stop because he was at his breaking point. He felt that he was ready to make it stop.

"Baby, what are you over here doing, huh?" Gloria asked, as she sat down beside Deron on his bed trying her best to act like everything in their lives was going great.

"Nothing momma, just looking outside." Deron replied, staring outside at the stars above. He loved to look at the sky at night and see the different alignment of the stars, wondering if he would ever be one them; a star.

"Baby, can momma talk to you for a second?"

"Yea momma, what about?" Deron asked. His eyes were squinted toward hers.

"Well, we hardly get a chance to sit down and talk." Gloria squeaked with a low tone. Deron wanted to be rude and give short, one word replies, but even though his mom was on drugs and he had all of this anger towards her, he still felt the need to respect her.

"Baby, I don't know if you started thinking about girls or not, but that time is coming."

"Momma, I can think about girls all I want, but no girls will be thinking about me because….." Deron stopped in mid sentence and looked away because he felt he was about to get rude and he told himself that he wouldn't do that.

"Momma, I'm just not thinking about girls right now."

"Well, baby I still have some things that I want you to know." Gloria said as she rested her hand on Deron's cold shoulder. He felt his blood boiling because of her touch, and he didn't understand why. Deron looked forward to his mom showing him any kind of affection and the fact that he was irritated by her touch, frustrated him more.

"Ok momma, what do you have to say?" Deron said in a spit-it-out kind of way.

"Can you please look at me at least?" Gloria said as she borderline shouted at her increasingly angry son. He huffed and turned towards her, hoping that she caught the hint that wasn't in the mood.

"Fine, I'm trying to talk to you baby, but it's clear that you don't want to talk to me right now, so I'll just leave, but can you please promise me something? As a matter of fact, I'm not asking you to promise me, I'm telling you to." Caught off guard by her orders, Deron perked up and his ears were opened to whatever Gloria had to say. He thought to himself, finally tell me what to do, he could and did respect that.

"Yes ma'am, I promise. What is it?" Deron begged. Gloria paused for awhile, took his nervous hand and just started crying. It used to hurt his heart to hear or see his mom crying, but Deron had grown accustomed to it. He got to the point that if she wasn't crying, something was wrong.

"Baby, I need you to promise that whatever you want, you go after it whole heartedly. If you love something, I mean you really love it, don't abuse it, and definitely don't take it for granted because this thing called love can leave in the blink of an eye. If you fall in love with a girl, you cherish her and make her feel like the only person in the world that exists. We all have flaws baby, if you love someone, then love them. If you fall out of love with them, let them go. I'll say this then I'll leave. Make your word mean something. If you say you're going to do something, you better make sure you do it. If you say you love something, you better make sure you love it. Now, momma gonna go, but if you remember nothing else I tell you, I hope you remember that."

Gloria said what she had to say and quickly walked out of Deron's dark room while he was still sitting there hanging onto the hope that she would tell him she loved him, but he sat there and wondered why she expressed to him what she did.

Gloria and Paul were up to their nightly fight and Deron laid there in his bed with the pillows covering his ears like headphones. He heard the constant banging of his mom hitting the floor and walls with Paul's persistent attempts of what he thought was him trying to kill Gloria. Deron's eyes were narrow and angled, his hands moved themselves into a fist and his teeth were grinding.

This was the first time that Deron thought that he wanted to kill his dad. He couldn't take it anymore so he did what he was sure Gloria was doing, he was crying.

Deron sat there looking out of the window and he eventually cried himself to sleep. Finally, morning had come and he no longer asked for a ride to school. He got up, dressed himself, fixed something to eat, walked out of the door, and he was on his way to school.

Deron thought a lot about what his mom had to say to him last night and he kept thinking about Janiya. She was the one person he kept thinking of when Gloria was talking. He thought about how much he loved her and how crazy it was that he loved her. Also, Deron thought about what she would do if she knew he even liked her and that's if she even knew he existed.

"What up blood?" A scraggly gang member said to Deron as he walked by. Deron just looked at him and looked away. The gang members wouldn't really do anything to him because they could see that he had nothing to offer them.

He wore torn up shoes and his pants sometimes barely reached his ankles. Holes in his shirts weren't a rare sight to see either. He wore the same black and purple Starter jacket for the last two years, so to attempt to jack him would be a waste of time and energy for them.

The prostitutes use to flirt with Deron, but now he figured he looked like he caught something worse than the disease he was sure they had. Deron's clothes may have been too small and had holes in them, but he made sure that they always stayed clean. He would wash his clothes in the middle of the night when Gloria cried herself to sleep from Paul beating on her and when his dad was passed out drunk.

Finally, Deron made it to school and before he walked through the door, he took a deep breath and said that today will be the day that he would speak to Janiya. There she was as Deron sauntered slowly into the building, looking as stunning as ever. She was alone and walking toward his direction. His heart raced, his breathing quickened and his cheeks were flushed in excitement. His palms shook nervously, but he was ready for the moment.

Her eyes sparkled and the waves in her hair flowed softly as she walked Deron's way, getting closer and closer. He watched her golden skin as she locked her fingers together. She wore a purple dress with a white flower band on her hair. Deron noticed her shiny white shoes and it seemed they were calling his name every time they hit the floor.

Janiya was getting closer and closer and closer to him. The closer she got, the more nervous he became. His hands were sweaty and for some reason he had a knot in his throat the size of a basketball.

Deron stood there as Janiya glided toward him and for that instant; she was the only person in his world that existed. He was ready and he told himself to relax and talk like he wanted to be heard. Girls like men that exude confidence and he was ready to show her that he had it. Janiya was about three feet from him and this was it. He spoke.

"Ummm…Hey….I….." The moment was gone. Janiya's friend, who Deron known to be named Layla, came

and turned her away from him and there she went, walking
away. Deron's head fell, his eyelids drooped and he remained
motionless.

Finally, he turned and walked away, and then he stopped
to turn around to catch another glimpse of the stunning
Janiya. She was walking away, but to his surprise, she turned
and looked directly at him. For the first time, their eyes
intentionally met each other's and it was confirmed, Deron
was in love.

The fact that she turned around to see him made his day.
Deron couldn't care less that Layla came and stole her away
because he spoke to her and his eyes met her hypnotizing
eyes. So far, this was the best day of his life and he had a
feeling it would get much better.

He was now determined to hear the sound of her voice.
He wanted to be able to put a sound to the songs that she
would sing to herself.

Deron was useless in class because he couldn't think
about anything except getting to recess to watch Janiya.
When the recess bell rang, he jumped out of his seat and
practically ran to recess.

"Man, where you going?" Christian asked. Christian
Roberts was one of if not the only good friend that Deron
had. He was a foster child and none of the other kids liked
him either so they kind of clicked. Christian stood a little
shorter than Deron and he was a little darker, but he was cool
to Deron.

"I'm going to recess." Deron replied with hurried words.

"Why you all in a rush to get there though?" Christian
asked. He was a cool kid to Deron, but he often asked too
many questions and sometimes it was funny and sometimes it
was just flat out frustrating. Like Gloria said, we all have our
flaws.

"You know that I have to get every moment I can to see Janiya, plus I don't wanna miss it if anyone tries to mess with her."

"Man, you ain't gon' do nothing if they do, but get beat up again. Anyway, why you seem a little bit more in a rush than usual? Why are you walking so fast Deron?" Christian chuckled while Deron almost ran into some lockers.

"You wouldn't understand if I told you Christian, trust me." Deron replied.

They were outside and Christian asked the frustrated Deron about twenty more questions and he just tuned him out until he finally got the hint and left to go play basketball. He sat in his normal seat on the bleachers while watching Janiya. She was so beautiful and she seemed so happy.

Deron just wanted to go right up to her and start talking. Janiya and Layla were on the swings when he noticed some boy go up to her. His eyes squinted trying to get focused on what was going on because it didn't look like Janiya was too happy.

She got up from the swings and walked away, but Layla and the boy followed. Deron's sweaty hands quickly became balled up fists. His jaws got tight when he saw Janiya's face because it definitely looked like trouble.

Layla and the boy were laughing, but Janiya wasn't too happy. The next thing Deron saw was Janiya hit the ground as the two walked away. Deron arose quickly to his feet and just like that, he was on his way over to Janiya.

Deron walked for what seemed like the length of a football field without blinking once. All the nervousness he ever had about approaching Janiya was gone and over because someone had physically hurt the girl he knew he loved. His eyes twitched in anger and his mouth began to snarl, but it all went away when he stood over Janiya and offered his hand.

"Are you okay?" Deron asked while still extending his hand out to Janiya. She looked at his hand and then up at him until she finally accepted it.

"Yes I'm okay I guess." Janiya replied. Her voice was so enchanting and her touch was so magnetic that Deron couldn't let go of her hand. Janiya stood up and brushed the dirt off of her dress and shook the dirt out of her hair.

"Why did you come over here? I didn't need any help." Janiya said without looking at Deron.

"Well, do you want the truth?" Deron asked.

"That would be nice."

"I saw that you were in danger and I don't like to see anything wrong with you." Deron was prepared to see Janiya's eye raise up and she would say, boy please, as she walked away, but instead she just stood there watching him.

"Well, my name is Janiya." She said while twirling strings of her hair around her fingers.

"Hi Janiya, my name is Deron, Deron Jamison and it's nice to finally meet you."

"Same here." Janiya replied back.

"So, why did that boy push you?" Deron asked as they sat next to each other on the swings.

"It's a long story and trust me; you don't want to hear me go on and on." Janiya said as she rolled her eyes his way and grinned softly.

"Do you see these? I think they work pretty well." Deron said as he pointed to his ears and for the first time, Deron saw Janiya laugh. She had the prettiest white teeth and a gorgeous set of deep dimples. She tried her best to cover up her smile with her hand, but he saw through it.

"Well, Mr. Deron, that girl over there is, or was, my best friend, Layla. That boy who pushed me is Tyler Jones." Janiya explained.

The smile that Deron had prior had disappeared once he heard that Tyler pushed her. Janiya kept talking and he kept

34

listening, but he was sure to keep Tyler in his sight. Janiya and Deron sat there talking for the rest of recess talking about their families until the bell rang for them to return to their class.

"It was really nice talking to you Deron and I hope we can talk some more and maybe become friends." Janiya said.

Deron just stared at her, waiting for this dream to be over with. She walked away after they shook hands and his eyes quickly went from a daze of love, to anger and fury with Tyler in his sights.

He made sure Janiya made it safely in the building and then he sprinted towards Tyler who was two grades ahead of him and about a half a foot taller. The angered Deron jumped on him and the fight was on. Deron punched Tyler and wouldn't stop swinging until someone tore him away from the bruised and badly beaten Tyler.

Deron's mission was to make everyone aware that Janiya was not to be touched. Tyler and Deron wrestled on the ground and he kept punching until he saw blood and even still, he did not stop until he felt the principal grab him by his collar and yank him off of Tyler.

Thirty minutes had gone by and Deron was sitting across from Tyler waiting in the principal's office for the paddling that we were going get.

"What is your problem homeless boy?" Tyler asked.

"You can call me whatever you want, but if you want this to be the last time you experience a busted lip and a black eye, I suggest you leave Janiya alone." Deron said, leaning forward with his eyes glued to Tyler. Deron meant business and soon everyone would know.

CHAPTER 5
1991 JANIYA 15 YEARS OLD

Janiya was laying in her princess style bed with the biggest smile on her face. She couldn't believe her and Deron had been talking every day since the day at the swings when he protected her from Tyler and Layla.

Deron found a way for them to talk every single day and Janiya loved that about him. She felt so protected just knowing that he was around and she felt protected when she would talk to him. Nothing in the world could mess with her and she loved that feeling. Since that day, she always thought about telling Deron she loved him.

He was her best friend and it was something about him that she found herself in love with, but she wasn't ready for him to know it yet. It was probably because Janiya didn't think he felt the same way about her and she didn't want to embarrass herself or mess up a good thing with a good friend.

Deron was smart, handsome, and a breath of fresh air. Everyone was quick to point out all of the things that he had going wrong in his life like his alcoholic dad and his crackhead mom.

Janiya often felt bad for him because he would come to school in clothes that she wouldn't even use as a Halloween costume. All of the kids talked bad about him, but one thing she loved about Deron was that he didn't care what people said about him, as long as they didn't touch him or harm her. Besides, Deron was good-looking to Janiya. She loved the way one side of his lips curled up when he tried not to smile. He had the cutest dimples that she had ever seen to go with his high cheek bones. He wasn't skinny, but he wasn't big either. Deron was perfect and his eyes were a brownish grey color with some green in it.

Janiya often found herself floating inside his eyes, trying her best to bring out some of the beauty that she saw in them. She continued to lie in her bed daydreaming about Deron until her mother interrupted her thoughts.

"Knock, knock, knock." Edna said while opening her door. She was dressed as if she's getting ready to go somewhere. She was clutching her shiny blue Coach purse and was dazzled up at 9:30 at night.

"Baby, I'm going to go to the store for your father, he's not feeling too well and we've already sent Lorretta home for the day." Edna said while coming to sit beside Janiya on her bed.

"Ok mother. So I'm going to be here by myself?" Janiya asked with a bothered look plastered on her depressing face. She sat up in her bed while pulling her hair back in a ponytail. "No silly, your father will be in our room until I get back. If you need anything, just go down and ask him. I won't be long."

Instantly, Janiya started to get chills and they weren't the same kind of chills she got when Deron crossed her mind.

She hated being alone with her step father and she expressed this to her mother plenty of times.

"Mother can you take me with you please?" Janiya fell to her knees as she begged and eventually crawled into her mother's lap.

"Mother, I'll do anything. Please don't make me stay here." Janiya cried in her mother's chest and she basically laughed at her begging attempts to be protected.

"Baby nothing is going to hurt you while your father is here." Edna stood up and pulled her blanket up to her chin to tuck Janiya in.

Janiya was still crying and she only wished Deron could help her. She watched her mother as she sauntered out of her room, but not before she cried out to her one last time to take her along with her. Edna ignored Janiya and shut her door saying that she will be home soon.

Just like that, her mother was gone and she was left feeling terrified in her bed. She shook nervously and couldn't control herself. Janiya would feel more comfortable if Loretta was there, but even she was blind when it comes to certain things about her family.

There were things that Lorretta understood about her family and there were things that Edna and Phillip refused to let her know about. They told Janiya not to tell her either, but the fearful child was getting closer and closer to telling Lorretta more about their so called "great" family.

For one, Phillip was not her biological father. Edna met him after her real dad was killed in a tragic car accident. Phillip Brakens was his name and he was actually the police officer that came and told Edna about the car accident.

Shortly after, they started dating and eventually they got married. Janiya was only three years old when all of that went down and she didn't remember too much. Edna demanded that she start calling Phillip, Mr. Brakens. Then later, she forced Janiya to start calling him father.

Phillip was a tall, mean, aggressive man. He demanded her mother do whatever he asked and he expected everything to go his way because he was the one bringing in all of the money. Janiya never really felt comfortable around Phillip and she hated being alone in the same room as he.

Their family had its secrets and Edna was naïve sometimes in hopes that they came off as the perfect family. Her job was to make sure everything in their house went smooth.

Janiya was afraid and Phillip sensed it, but he never cared. She didn't like him and felt that he didn't like her either.

After a few minutes, she finally had cried herself to sleep. The tears had dried up on her face and her ponytail had become the pillow to some of her fallen tears. She had fallen asleep in hopes that she wouldn't awaken until the sunshine opened her eyes.

"Wake up baby." Janiya thought she felt mother waking her up, but she still wanted to stay asleep.

"Come on baby, get up."

"Mother!" Janiya screamed as she popped up from her sleep.

"I'm sorry, I know I look a little feminine at times baby girl, but I'm not your mother. Why do you look so scared of your father baby girl? I'm just coming up here to check on you." Phillip said while cracking a sarcastic smirk.

"Father, what are you doing in my room? I was sleep!" Janiya screamed while backing away from him since he sat close up on her.

"Now Janiya, is that anyway to speak to your father? As a matter of fact, I'm not your father so just call me Phil or Phillip, which ever you prefer." Phillip said as he grinned.

He turned to face her and his eyes moved over the frightened Janiya, which made her very uncomfortable. She pulled her blanket closer to her and begged for Phillip to leave her room, but he just laughed it off.

"Father, what do you want? Please leave, please!" Tears started falling from her eyes while shouting for Phillip to leave.

"Aww baby girl, I told you to call me Phillip. I won't hurt you. I just came up here to make sure you were ok." Phillip reached his hand out to wipe her tears away. She flinched as his huge hands moved closer to her and she tried backing away, but there was nowhere else to go.

"Relax baby girl and come to Phillip, I'll make you feel better." Phillip marched closer to Janiya and grabbed her, hurting her thin arms. He let her arms go and then started rubbing his hands on her head. Again, Janiya tried in vain to break away, but Phillip wasn't having it.

It was dark in her room and all she could see was Phillip's eyes. She couldn't see too much of anything else because he turned off all of her night lights while she was asleep. Janiya was afraid of the dark and her mom often joked about her growing up, still in need of a night light.

Phillip's eyes blinked rapidly and he kept licking his lips. His rough hands kept stroking his double chin with a silly grin planted on his bearded face.

"Baby girl come give me a hug since I don't feel too good. Yea, I think I need a hug from my baby girl." Phillip said as he held out his arms waiting on her to give him a hug.

"Phillip, no! Please leave my room, please!" Janiya screamed. Phillip put his arms down, closed his eyes and then glanced over at Janiya, shaking his head.

"Wrong answer baby girl. Wrong fucking answer. After all the shit I do for you and yo' stupid ass mother, you sit here and fucking disrespect me like this. I asked yo' stupid, ugly ass for a muthafuckin hug and you tell me no!" Veins were exploding from the heated Phillip. Janiya screamed while he continued his rant in hopes someone would hear her. Phillip jumped on top of her and there they were, wrestling around in her bed.

"Phillip, please get off of me!" Janiya screamed to the top of her lungs, but no one could hear her cries.

"We about to see if yo' stuff is as good as yo' mother's." Phillip said as he forced his tongue in Janiya's mouth. She slapped Phillip a few times but he laughed it off. She tried escaping a few times, but didn't get far. He made her think she was escaping, but he always came to get her and threw her back in the bed.

He was touching places that they both knew he shouldn't have been touching and he held the weak Janiya down as he took off his pants. Janiya closed her eyes and swung hopelessly at Phillip, eager that she would hit him enough until he backed away, but he kept coming.

Janiya grabbed anything that she could get her hands on to hit Phillip with. She threw any and everything at him to get him off of her, from her toys to her piggybank.

Twenty minutes later, Phillip rose up off of Janiya and looked outside her window. Her body laid there limp and she gazed into her ceiling fan. Not sure of what had just happened to her. Tears seemed to crawl slowly off of her face.

She knew she had just been molested, but wasn't sure on how to process it all. Janiya continued to lay there while Phillip jumped up quickly and put his pants on, running to her door. He turned back around, ran back up to her face. He had anger in his eyes. Sweat was running down his face, she took her hand and scratched him as hard as she could on his neck so mother would see it. Phillip responded with a powerful strike back across her face, so powerful that Janiya saw tears departing from his hands.

"Look you little bitch. If you tell your mother anything that happened here, I will kill you both. You should be happy I gave you a little something because yo' ugly ass wasn't gonna get it from no other guy. You're too ugly for anybody to want to be with you. Remember what I said. If anyone find out about this, you'll be sorry."

Janiya was in her room crying and scared because of what she knew Phillip would do to her. She buried her head in her hands and her hair was all over her head from fighting with Phillip. Again, Phillip ran to the doorway and stopped, he saw Janiya sitting there shaking and scared, but he didn't care.

"I know yo' stupid ass mother is gonna come up here to check on you so you better gone and pretend you're sleep." Phillip said as he stood in her doorway.

"Gone bitch, act like you sleep. I ain't playing with you." He slammed her door shut and Janiya was lying in her bed crying her eyes out. She couldn't believe what just happened. She always knew that there was a reason why she was scared to be alone with Phillip.

CHAPTER 6
1991 DERON 15 YEARS OLD

A whole year had passed since Janiya and Deron started talking that beautiful day at the swings. Since that day, no one had touched Janiya and that was exactly the way he wanted it. They talked everyday at school, weekends and over the summer break.

Deron would find a pay phone and call Janiya on her own phone line. Anytime he needed to talk about his busted family, she was there to listen and anytime she needed to know that someone didn't care how rich her family was, Deron was there for her.

Janiya and Deron somehow became best friends which frustrated a lot of people at school, but they were scared to say anything to Janiya about it because of the reputation Deron had built for himself.

Deron often felt that he existed only to protect Janiya and in no way was that a bad thing.

"Good morning Janiya." Deron said, happy to see her as she walked through the school doors. He went from happy to mad because Janiya walked right passed him and didn't notice him at all.

"Hello, Janiya." Deron said again as I walked up to her and tugged her shoulder. She jumped as if she just saw a ghost.

"Don't touch me." She cried and shouted while walking away. Immediately, Deron knew something was wrong and he was determined to find out. He couldn't focus in class and his feet tapped tensely alongside the poles of the desk. His fingers beat hard and fast waiting for the lunch bell to ring. His eyes couldn't tear away from the clock.

Finally, twelve o'clock came and Deron sprang out of his seat and ran to lunch. He went to their spot and waited for Janiya, but she never showed up so he walked around looking for her. It was no hope; he couldn't find Janiya anywhere and his heart felt like it had exploded.

Deron walked around wearing a frown on his face and wrinkles planted in forehead. The muscles in his throat were constricted and he was repeatedly swallowing all hope of finding where Janiya was.

Deron saw Layla and asked if she had seen her, but she just looked him up and down, basically ignoring Deron. Ten minutes were left during lunch and Deron finally saw Janiya hiding and crying.

"Janiya, what's wrong? Talk to me." Deron begged.

"Deron, you wouldn't understand. I just want to be left alone right now." Janiya said sniffling.

"Janiya, I'm not going to leave you. Just talk to me. I promise that it will make you feel better." Janiya stayed quiet and just stayed under the bleachers crying. He felt so bad and his heart was hurting for her.

Tears ran down the sides of Janiya's face, but she was still beautiful in the eyes of Deron. Her nose was red from the constant wiping and rubbing and her legs were crossed Indian style.

"Janiya, do you mind if I join you under here?" Deron asked. She shook her head no while still crying. Deron crawled under the bleachers and just held Janiya. He felt as though he was being selfish because he needed to hold her more than she needed to be held.

It was confusing to Deron how once he started holding Janiya, she started crying more. He thought he was doing it wrong, but she kept her head buried in his chest and just cried until she fell asleep.

Deron held Janiya tight until school was out and neither was bothered that they skipped their classes. Deron was only focused on Janiya and making sure she was ok. Janiya was held close and tight in his and no one could pry her away from him, not even her own thoughts.

Deron's shirt lay pressed to his chest from the tears that Janiya shed and his lower back was in knots from sitting in one position for so long. Every part of Deron was sore except his heart. It was only slightly bruised because of the hurt that Janiya felt and as he watched her green eyes slowly open.

Rubbing her eyes, Janiya jumped up and dusted herself off vigorously while avoiding hitting her head on the bleachers. Deron still saw hurt in her eyes as she wouldn't allow herself to make eye contact with him. Her head stayed lowered and her once straight perfect posture was slumped in embarrassment.

"Janiya?" Deron called her name and prayed she would answer, but she just got her things and walked out from under the bleachers. He followed and continued to call her name until she reached her ride home.

"Thank you for holding me Deron, but I have to leave now." Janiya said without even turning in his direction. He watched as she hopped in the back seat and slammed the door shut. They drove away and Janiya's head stayed slumped. Deron's heart was broken.

Torey Irving

It was Friday night and Deron couldn't stop thinking about what happened earlier at school with Janiya. It felt like heaven when he held Janiya, but only for a split second, because he knew the reason he was holding her had some hell involved somewhere.

He desperately needed to talk to Janiya and he needed her to want to talk to him about what was going on. Deron was willing to make that happen any way possible.

Tip toeing to his bedroom door, he opened it slowly and prayed that the squeaking wouldn't wake Paul up from his drunken coma. He knew Gloria would be asleep even though it was only seven o'clock. So he walked through the dark hallway with his hands holding on to the filthy walls. The same walls that were filled with remnants of Gloria's blood, from all the beatings she took.

Deron kept looking back just in case Paul had awakened. His heart was pounding so hard that he heard it beating him upside his head. It seemed like a scene straight from a movie.

All of the lights in the house were out except the flickering light in the bathroom. Water dripped endlessly from the kitchen sink begging Deron to retrace his steps and rethink this thing through. He had come too far to turn back.

Deron footsteps were halted when he heard Paul coughing. He stood motionless, hoping the crease from the moon didn't give him away. He had a simple plan, but the execution of the plan was kicking his ass right now.

His plan was to sneak out of the house and somehow break into the school to get Janiya's address. He would then find a phone to call Janiya even though he doubted she would answer.
Coming up with the plan was the easy part to Deron; the hard part was putting it all together. The palms of his hands were clammy and his eyes were continuously moving. He

wondered what the hell he was doing, but his heart answered the question for him.

Quietly, he opened the door to Gloria's room and she was passed out on floor. Her hair was tangled around her face and her arms were thrown across her chest lifeless. Gloria's snores were the only hint to Deron that she was still alive because the rest of her seemed deceased.

Everything was going good until Deron Paul was walking toward the bathroom.

"What the hell you doing up boy? Yo' crackhead momma don't wanna see you." Paul said with his raspy voice. His eyes were glazed and just as Deron was about to respond, Paul shut the door in his face. He was actually glad that he did because it made it that much easier for Deron to sneak out of the house.

Deron had never been more scared in his life than he was at that moment. He had to walk the streets of Oak Cliff, which is on the borderline of South Dallas, and that's even worse. His fist stayed balled up just in case someone, or something ran up on him. His head never dropped. To be from that part of Dallas, Deron had to learn certain things that's was key to survival.

If someone made eye contact with Deron, he stared them down and made sure his eyes wasn't the first to redirect. It was a mind thing for him also because he hated losing at anything. It was easier if he made things a contest. Deron learned to stop walking around with his head down because it signified softness and he knew he wasn't soft.

Lions were his favorite animal and he often thought of himself as a lion, the king of the jungle. Many fights came Deron's way because of his demeanor, but his demeanor also kept him from some fights. Being 15 years old, Deron got tried a lot, but his reputation grew from a little homeless boy with a crackhead momma, to the little ass cool kid with heart.

"What up blood?" A gang member said as he gave Deron the head nod.

"Sup?" Deron replied and kept walking.

"Hold up, hold up." He said while walking Deron's way. He was a tall, black guy and was wearing baggy, black clothes with a red bandanna hanging out of his pocket. Deron tried to look past the tattoos that he had on his face, the gold chains he wore, but he was standing right in front of him, so it was hard to miss.

"Whatchu doing round here youngsta?"

"Man what's yo' name?" Deron courageously asked, pretending he wasn't asked a question first.

"Who wants to know lil nigga?" He yelled back.

"You asking me questions, why can't I ask you some questions?" Deron's fists were perspiring and his heart was beating fast. His eyes stayed narrow and never left the guy's face.

"Yall come get a look at lil dude. He tryna act all hard and shit." He laughed to his friends. They all laughed and came up circling the calm Deron.

"Now, I'ma ask you on more time potna. Whatchu doing round here youngsta?"

"Man, you can keep asking me, but I'm gon' keep asking you the same question. What's your name? Bruh?" Deron replied back while staring him dead in the eyes. He knew the gang member was because his boy's starting laughing at him, which didn't make things any better.

"Lil homie, all that was good at first, but now you being a lil disrespectful. Don't you know what we can do to you right about now potna?" He said while jumping in Deron's face.

"Look at me man. I'm a 15 year old kid with busted up clothes, my pops is an alcoholic, my moms is a crackhead. Shit, they don't even know that I'm out, well let me rephrase that, they don't care that I'm out. So do it look like I can give a damn what y'all can do to me? Whatever it is, trust me, you'll be doing me a favor, so gon' and get it over with." The gang members all just stood there not really knowing what to do.

"Aight, since y'all just gon' stand there and look at me crazy, I'm gon' walk off and y'all can choose to do whatever y'all want to me, but I got bidness to tend to, so I'll be on my way. Holla." And just like that, Deron was back on his journey to the school house praying that the gang members didn't choose to do something to him, because he knew he definitely had it coming.

Deron walked past a few more gang members and prostitutes before finally making it to the school and luckily, he didn't run into problems with anyone. About twenty minutes later Deron was inside the school building trying to hurry up and find the admissions office. He wore all black just in case there were cameras watching him. He knew that they wouldn't check the cameras as long as nothing strange happened.

Deron had other things to do besides get Janiya's address and he was ready to get on with it. Before leaving his house, he filled a bag full of dead rats and roaches that resided in his home and he put them in every kids locker that messed with Janiya, and wrote a note that simply said "Stop fucking with her or next time, I will make you eat it." Now, on to the office. Deron walked the halls as carefully as possible, but stayed buried against the walls as he continued. There were no security guards because no one was capable, or smart enough, to come and try to secure this neighborhood and Deron didn't blame them.

Finally, he made it to the office and things were working in his favor because the door was left unlocked. He turned the knob, slow as possible, Deron was in. He worked his way around the office trying to locate where they kept the files, but he was competing with the darkness.

Deron searched for about an hour and finally found Janiya's file. Got it, 3254 South Maragos Court in Lancaster, TX. It was a ways from where he was, so he searched some of the desk around him until he found a good chunk of money to catch a cab. Making sure everything was back the way he found it, Deron hurried out of the school building and called a taxi. Twenty minutes later, he was on his way to Janiya's.

CHAPTER 7

Janiya

It was late and there was no way that Janiya could get some sleep after what Phillip had done to her the night before. She was still in shock and hadn't spoken one word to anyone other than the few words she uttered to Deron.

Janiya replayed that whole night over and over in her head and she didn't know why because obviously, she wished it had never happened. She remembered everything that Phillip done. Every word that he spoke and she didn't think she would ever forget them.

Janiya wanted so badly to tell her mother, but she clearly remember Phillip threatening to kill them both if she said anything, so she stayed quiet.

Telling Lorretta was an option, but Janiya knew that Phillip would kill her too. The safest person that she could tell seemed to be Deron, but she wasn't sure she wanted Deron knowing that.

Edna tried speaking to Janiya a few times today, but Phillip made sure that he was always around. He watched her closely out the corners of his evil eyes. Making sure that she gave no hints to Edna as to what happened.

Janiya stayed in her room the entire time since coming home from school. She assumed it would be a long night, being terrified of falling asleep.

Slowly, Janiya was starting to believe everything that Phillip said about her. She was starting to believe that she was ugly and no boy in school wanted to be around her. Even though Deron said that he loved to be around her, he's the only one. Her best friend, Layla turned on her and basically turned everyone against her since she started talking to Deron.

Janiya tried wiping away the tears from her eyes, but she couldn't wipe fast enough. She tried her best to lie down and force herself to sleep. It was impossible because every time she shut her eyes, she saw Phillip forcing himself inside her and it was a continuous nightmare.

Janiya finally had forced herself to sleep, but was awaken by a sound at her window. She wiped away the sleep from her heavy eyes and couldn't believe what she saw when she sat up and looked in the direction of her window. Was it a dream? Janiya asked herself.

It was Deron, what was he doing there? How did he get there? Janiya continue to ask herself the rhetorical questions. She couldn't believe it and was so shocked that she didn't even go over to open the window. She stayed there in her bed with a silly smile on her face.

Finally, she hurried out of her bed and ran over to the window. Janiya was looking out at Deron and couldn't believe how handsome he looked to her. He was dressed in all black and sweat beaded down his caramel skin like the rain falling from heaven. His eyes twinkled in the moonlight and Janiya knew she was in love. That made her feel like she was in hell because Phillip made her think she was incapable of being loved in return.

In her eyes, she was everything Phillip said she was and it wasn't only Phillip. Layla and other kids at school told her she was ugly and they made fun of her freckles. So she started to believe what she was hearing. Deron was motioning the sleep deprived Janiya to open the window. She followed his instructions, but she knew she needed to be careful because Lorretta was still there. Janiya wasn't sure if Edna and Phillip were still up so she quietly opened the window.

"Deron, what are you doing here?" Janiya asked, trying her best to whisper.

"I just wanted to make sure you were ok Janiya. I know something is bothering you and it's killing me." Deron replied while inches away from Janiya.

"Janiya, is there somewhere we could talk?" Deron asked.

"Yea, gimme one second, I'ma see if my parents are still up." She motioned for Deron to hide until she came back so he hid under Janiya's bed until she returned.

Janiya was still in shock that he was there, but she was thrilled to know end, to see him. She tip toed quickly to her door and walked downstairs pretending that she needed a drink of water. It seemed that her parents were asleep because most of the lights were off and no one was in sight. She continued to walk around until she got to the kitchen.

"Freeze young lady. What do you think you're doing?" It was Lorretta thank God. She made Janiya spill water on her night gown, but it was much better than Phillip finding her down there.

"Umm Lorretta, you scared me." Janiya replied while trying to wipe away some of the water that spilled on her.

"Chica, I thought you were sleep, what are you still doing up?" Lorretta asked as she stood there smiling at Janiya with her hands on her perfectly shaped hips. She was so beautiful to Janiya and she always felt that Lorretta could be a model. She was gorgeous and Janiya really looked up to her.

"I came down for a drink of water Lorretta." Janiya stuttered. She knew she couldn't be down here long because Deron was still up in her room waiting on her to come back.

"Lorretta, are my parents sleeping?" Janiya asked while praying that they were.

"No chika, your parents went out tonight. Your mommy came up to your room, but she said you were sleep." Lorretta said as she cleaned up the mess Janiya made.

"Will they be gone long?" Janiya asked while leaning against the counter drinking her new glass of water.

"I believe so because they were dressed pretty fancy." That was all the information Janiya needed to know.

"Well Lorretta, thank you for cleaning my mess up for me, but I'm gonna go back to bed now. I just needed a drink of water." Janiya walked off with the cup of water and didn't look back.
"Call me on the intercom next time Janiya if you need anything, I don't mind." Lorretta said as she walked off. Janiya gave her the "ok" sign and continued back upstairs. Once she was out of Lorretta's sight, she practically ran upstairs to her room and locked the door behind her, just in case Lorretta came up to her room while she was talking to Deron.

Janiya looked everywhere for Deron and couldn't find him and suddenly he appeared behind her.

"Deron, where did you come from? I thought you were under the bed." Janiya's heart was beating fast and her hands began to shake. She still couldn't wipe away the smile that was painted on her face. Seeing Deron made her forget everything that was going on.

"I hid in the bathroom instead. Janiya, I can't believe you have a bathroom in your own room. That's crazy!" Deron said in amazement.

"How did you know where I stayed?" Janiya asked as her eyes pierced into Deron.

"Come on Janiya, we've been talking everyday for about a year and then all of sudden you don't talk to me and you start crying at recess. I know something is wrong with you and I came all the way over here to make sure you were ok. Can you talk?" Deron asked in a cool demanding way. Not too many people went out of their way to make sure Janiya was ok, well not too many people that wasn't paid to do it.

"You didn't answer my question, but that's ok. Umm...Deron...I don't know if I'm ok." Janiya couldn't stop twirling and fiddling with her hair, which was a habit she had.

Janiya's heart started to beat faster and faster. She kept looking behind her and didn't know why because her door was locked. She was just nervous and afraid because she never had a boy in her room. Deron wasn't just any boy to her, he was something special and that added to the nervousness she felt.

Janiya knew she was in love with him and honestly, she didn't see why he insisted on being around her. Even though on the outside looking in, people would say that she was too good for Deron, Phillip made her so insecure of herself and of her body. She felt Deron was too good for her and she didn't deserve to be in his presence.

"Janiya, can we go somewhere to sit and talk?" Deron asked and she couldn't say no to him once he looked her in the eyes. Janiya knew he couldn't stay long, but she walked him over to a corner in her room that she loved to go read. They both sat and began to talk.

"Yea but we will have to be quiet. You can sit right there." Janiya pointed to her purple chair next to her vanity set.

Deron and Janiya continued to talk for hours and she can honestly say that she hadn't had that much fun in a long time. Deron told her everything about his family and she felt bad for him because he felt no one cared about him.

She saw how much it hurt him to tell her that his parents didn't care if he even came home or not. Janiya started to see a different side of Deron that night and something made her want to cry for him. He was a good kid born into the wrong family. Deron could have easily gotten caught up in gangs, but he wanted no parts of it.

Majority of the time, Janiya had her head down because she couldn't bring herself to tell Deron what Phillip had done to her. So she mostly listened to Deron and kept things about her family short and sweet.

Deron was the perfect gentleman and they both knew that eventually, she would have to talk about what happened to her the other night, but Deron didn't force it, he let it happen on its own.

"Janiya I love your room, except for all the pinks and purples." They both laughed as Deron walked around her room inspecting everything.

"Wow, I can't believe how big your room is. Almost my whole apartment can fit in your room alone."

"Having everything does not mean you always have everything Deron. People may think I have it all, but they are sadly mistaken." Deron put down a magazine that he had picked up and sat beside Janiya on her bed.

She couldn't help, but lay her head on his chest like she did under the bleachers earlier.

"Deron?"

"Yea Janiya?" Deron spoke in a soft tone as Janiya felt his voice tremble through his chest.

"Do you wish sometimes your dreams were a reality and reality was your dreams?"

"Actually Janiya, I wish had dreams. I've had nightmares for the longest. Shit, I'm living a nightmare." Janiya felt Deron shaking his head as he finished speaking. It got quiet for a few minutes and Janiya kept her head pressed against Deron's chest. Their heart beats were in sync with each other's and to Janiya; it felt like they were on a beach alone listening to the waves of the ocean.

She so badly wanted to soak in the waves of Deron's love and let him deep dive in the essence of her heart. It was so relaxing, so peaceful and so tranquil, she just found herself slowly dozing off.

"Deron?"

"Yea?"

"Do you need to leave?" Janiya asked with her eyes still closed.

"No Janiya, I don't have to go anywhere. I want to stay here with you and make sure you're ok." Deron's answer brought a smile to Janiya's face and her heart. She had never been as peaceful as she was lying on Deron's chest.

"Deron?"

"Yea?" Deron laughed.

"What's so funny?" Janiya chuckled back.

"I just like how you say my name when you're about to ask me a question. I like that you ask questions. If you didn't realize it before, small things will win me over."

"Umm…I don't know how to really ask you this, but…"

"Janiya, don't ever be afraid to tell me something or ask me anything, even if you think it may hurt me."

"Do you believe in love Deron?" Janiya felt Deron take a hard swallow and he paused before answering her.

"I hate to answer a question with a question Janiya, but can you believe in something you know nothing about? If I had to answer, I guess I would say that I want to believe in it, but I don't think love or anyone believes in me." The moon shined right through her window and bounced right off the side of Deron's face. Janiya looked at him and he was starring out into open air, slowly a tear fell from his eyes.

"I believe in you Deron." Janiya whispered as she wiped away his tears, but they just kept coming and slowly, tears started to plummet down Janiya's face.

"Deron?"

"Yea?" Deron tried his best to hold in his laugh, but he sniffed out a grin anyway.

She was finally ready to tell Deron that she loved him and she didn't care if he didn't say it back. She loved him for a long time and other than what Phillip did to her the other day, this had been the best year of her young life.

Janiya was only 15 years old, but she knew she couldn't see herself living without Deron. She felt protected when she was around him and even when she wasn't, he seemed to always know when she was in danger and he'd find a way to come rescue her.

She was also ready to tell Deron about Phillip, had her reservations because she had no idea how Deron would react. So, she thought long and hard about if she was really ready to tell it all to.

What if he got grossed out by what Phillip did and never wanted to talk to her again? What if Deron only wanted to be her friend and had no thoughts of being in love with her? All of those questions crossed her mind, but she no longer cared. Deron had been honest with her about his family, so it was her turn to be honest about some things.

"I have to tell you something and I don't want you to get angry with me. Well, actually I have a few things that I've wanted to tell you and I just feel like getting it off my chest now."

"Ok Janiya what is it?"

"Well, I just want to tell you that…"

"Janiya, why is your door locked?" Lorretta screamed as she knocked on the door just as Janiya opened her mouth to speak to Deron.

"Janiya, open the door. Now!" Lorretta kept screaming. Deron and Janiya both shot up from the bed and neither one of them knew what to do. Lorretta continued to bang on her door.

"Janiya, I know someone is in your room. Open this door up now or I will tell your parents!" Deron and Janiya looked at each other and the one thing that she loved about Deron was one thing she came to hate also. He was so brave, but sometimes she didn't want him to be brave and this was one of those times Janiya wanted Deron to be scared out of his mind and jump out of the window.

"Janiya, open the door. No one is gonna hurt you. Trust me!" Deron was all of sudden calm and cool while Janiya was a nervous wreck. Her hands had worked themselves through her hair and practically took apart her ponytail. Deron stood there with his head held high gesturing for Janiya to open the door. After stalling, she finally gave in and opened the door.

"Hi, my name is Deron. I'm one of Janiya's schoolmates and I'm sorry I'm here at this time of night, but I felt something was wrong with Janiya and I wanted to check on her. Please forgive me ma'am." Janiya's feet were cemented to the floor as she wondered what the hell Deron was doing.

"Hi Deron, my name is Lorretta. I'm Janiya's nanny and I appreciate your concern, but you can't be here." Lorretta said while glaring at Janiya.

Janiya didn't like what Deron did, but he definitely calmed Lorretta down. He was so cool under pressure that she was amazed.

"Deron, how did you get here and where do you stay?" Lorretta asked as she fully walked into Janiya's dark room and looked her over to see if she was ok.

"I got here by taxi ma'am and I stay in Oak Cliff."
Deron replied. He spoke with such calmness and confidence.
There was no stutter in his words and no tremble in his voice.
He stood tall and never took his eyes away from Lorretta, no
matter how many times she looked at him and broke away to
check on Janiya.

They all stood there with Janiya watching Lorretta,
Lorretta watching Deron, and Deron watching Lorretta as
well.

"Well Janiya, your parents are on their way back to the
house and Deron, you can't be here when they get back."

"I understand ma'am, I just wanted to make sure Janiya
was ok. I'll be leaving now." Deron strutted up to Lorretta
and shook her hand, turned back to Janiya and gave her the
biggest hug that she's ever gotten and proceeded to crawl out
of the window.

"Wait! Deron I can't have you taking a taxi back to Oak
Cliff at this time of night." Lorretta said.

"It's no big deal ma'am, trust me I'll be fine. Trust me."

"I'm sure you will be, but I'm going to take you home.
Now say good bye to Janiya and go wait in my car until her
parents get home, then I will take you back to your house."
Lorretta said as she stood in the doorway. She pointed to her
watch signaling for Deron to speed up his goodbye.

"Well Janiya, this was the best night of my life. I just
love to talk to you. What were you going to tell me?"

"Don't worry about it Deron, I'll tell you Monday at
school because I don't have enough time to tell you now."
Deron finally dropped his head. Janiya could tell he was
disappointed and it seemed that he was hurt at the same time.
She's never known someone that actually took pride in
hearing what she had to say the way Deron did. He always
made hre feel like she was the only person in the world that
existed. For a spoiled rich kid like herself, that was
important.

"Ok Janiya, I'll see you Monday." Deron said as he hugged Janiya and tears nearly ran out of her eyes when she saw Deron walk away.

Lorretta closed the door and something didn't feel right about seeing Deron walk away from her. Worrisome chills started to envelop her body and her heart felt like it was about to jump out of her chest. She felt it and she wondered if Deron felt it also.

CHAPTER 8

Deron

Deron couldn't help but to keep letting his eyes bounce back to Janiya's window. Thinking to himself that he wished he was still there. There was an unsettling feeling that he had and as Lorretta opened the door to her fancy car. Deron turned, looked up to Janiya's window one last time. There was no sight of her.

The bright lights shone in his face while the trees cut into the moonlight. Deron felt like just like that moonlight and Loretta was the trees that cut through the light that he tried to shine on Janiya.

"Buckle up Deron and try to stay awake back there, so you can help me get to your house." Lorretta said with a thick accent.

She kept trying to talk to Deron, but all she got were some head nods and some mmm's and yes ma'am's. Lorretta's car made it easy for Deron to doze off. It felt better than anything inside his house and anything that he's ever sat on. The leather seats combined with the cool AC told Deron to go to sleep, but thinking about Janiya kept him awake.

He kept thinking and wondering what it was that she had to tell him. It would continue to eat away at Deron's mind like an ant destroying food at a picnic. He always had the tendency to over think things and he hated having to wonder about anything.

Janiya was his best friend, his everything and he almost couldn't breathe right without knowing.

Lorretta spoke his name in a cool and calm voice and he loved the feeling of hearing his name being spoken like that. He was so used to hearing his name being yelled and screamed out.

"So Deron?" Lorretta spoke, but he tried his best to pretend he was sleep. However, he also wanted her to keep saying his name. Her loved her accent, she said his name while rolling the "r's" and for some reason, it put him in a comfortable place.

"Come on Deron, I know you're not sleep papi, I see your little eyes fighting to stay open." Lorretta said with a slight smile.

"Fine, I'm not sleep, but I'm just worried, that's all." Deron said, finally rising from a laying position on the cool, leather back seat. Deron was confused because he was so used to being uncomfortable, but there he was, totally comfortable.

"So Deron, you like my little Janiya, yes?" Deron couldn't believe she asked him that, just straight out. Instantly and nervously, his heart started racing because on the inside, he was screaming out "Yes! Hell Yes!! I love Janiya!" but of course he didn't want anyone to know it.

Deron was sure Janiya liked him as a friend and if that's all she wants from him, he'd gladly take that in a split second. His eyes and shoulders dropped in embarrassment and he started stuttering.

"N..no..ummm no, I don't.....I don't like her. I...I mean yes I...."

"Calm down Deron, I didn't ask you if you wanted to marry her. I just asked if you like her and I already know you do. No one comes all the way 'cross town just to check on someone unless they really like them. It's ok, you can tell me papi, I won't tell anyone."

"Yes, I like Janiya as a friend." That was Deron's story and he was sticking to it. They went back and forth for another ten minutes. She continued to try and make him say that he liked Janiya as a girlfriend. He couldn't and wouldn't give in when he knew Janiya didn't feel the same about him. It was understandable to Deron; he was a borderline homeless kid with no goals and nothing in life.

Deron basically live for Janiya's happiness and to him that was worth living. That was his million dollars and that was his every reason for wanting to live. The way she smiled made Deron weak and made him melt. Every time she smiled, she showed those pearly white teeth with a dimple on her left cheek. Deron always felt the need to go diving in it, it was so deep. He kept daydreaming about Janiya and he wondered if Loretta knew it because she was quiet the rest of the way.

"Miss Loretta, you can make a right up here and then a left onto Overton Road. You will see my apartments."

"Ok papi." Loretta said. Deron couldn't wait to get home and go to sleep and wait for his chance to see Janiya at school again. He couldn't stop thinking about what she wanted to talk to him about. If he could, he would sneak back over to her house, once Loretta dropped him off.

"Papi!" Loretta screamed. Deron immediately looked up and there were policeman, fire trucks and ambulances parked in his apartment complex which was a normal. He could definitely understand why Loretta freaked out.

"Papi, what's going on?" Loretta asked as if he knew something she didn't.

"Relax Miss Loretta, I'll be worried if a day comes where the police didn't show up." Loretta laughed as the lights from the paramedics bounced off of her face.

"Well thank you Miss Loretta for the ride home, I really appreciate it. I do hope I didn't upset you too much back there. I just really needed to see Janiya." Deron said before hopping out of smooth-riding car.

"No, problem papi and don't worry, I won't tell Janiya that you like her." Loretta said with the biggest smile.

"Now go on up to your house and I will wait down here until I see you go in."

At that moment, Deron was so happy and slightly jealous of Janiya. Lorretta was so thoughtful, so caring and he was so excited that Janiya had this kind of person always around her. He was also slightly jealous because he wanted that for himself as well.

Deron never had anyone care enough about his well being and his was hesitant to walk away so quickly from it. He finally walked away, but turned back to wave at Lorretta. He could see her smiling, even through the raindrops that started to find a home onto her windows.

There was a creepy chill in the air as Deron hurried himself up to his apartment building. He dodged all of the people and police officers that flooded near his building.

"Deron, baby, come here." Miss Velma said as her hands covered her tear stained face. Deron stopped and just watched Miss Velma. She had her torn up house shoes on with her house coat on. She tried to hold it together once she dropped her hands from her face. Her eyes displayed of sorrow and hurt, and her lips were trembling, shaking as she tried her best to speak again.

"Deron, baby, come here to Miss Velma." She pleaded again.

"Miss Velma, I have to get in the house before momma and daddy wake up. Why are you crying?" Deron asked, knowing he wouldn't like the answer. He knew something wasn't right, but he wasn't ready to face something tragic. He felt that if assumed everything was fine, then it would be.

Deron kept walking towards his apartment and Miss Velma plastered her hands on her face again, crying uncontrollably. At that moment, he knew something bad had happened. He wondered if his mom finally fought back. Or were they on their way to jail again? Deron gave a final wave to Miss Lorretta as she stood in the crowded parking lot. Street lights and flashing police lights beamed down on everyone. Finally, Deron walked inside his apartment, and there was Paul.

"Hey hey there son, come on over here with your dad." Paul of course was drunk again, his eyes hung low, and his speech was slurred. In other words, everything was normal except for the gun that he waved around.   The police officer stood there yelling for Deron to move and he remember thinking to himself that the officer didn't have to worry about that. Deron scanned the filthy apartment in search of his mother. Clothes were thrown everywhere, lamp shades laid wrongly against the couch while the lamp let out more light than normal. Broken dishes made their mark up against the filthy walls of dirt and cigarette marks from when Paul refused to use an astray.

There were no signs of Gloria anywhere and Deron wanted desperately to find out where she was. Seeing the officer's gun drawn and Paul waving his gun carelessly, made Deron decide otherwise.

"Hey son, come over here, didn't you hear me the first time?" Paul said while his eyes were halfway open. He spoke as if he was slinging his indistinct words at Deron.

"Dad, what are you doing and where is momma?"

"Shit son, I don't know where that crack head bitch is, shit!" Paul said. Deron finally saw his mom and if Miss Velma had seen her, she would say "Baby you look like hell."

Blood cascaded down her face and she had holes ripped in her clothes to the point where her bra was barely hanging on.

Deron couldn't believe what was going on and Gloria came walking from the back room like nothing was wrong, fixing her clothes as if she getting ready to model.

"Come here baby." Gloria said trying her best to sound normal.

"Stay your crackhead ass back, I don't have a problem pulling this trigger. Now son get yo' ass over here, I won't tell you again!" Paul said while blowing cigarette smoke in his direction.

"Put the gun down sir!" The officer screamed, but Paul pointed his gun and puffed on his cigarette. The smoke filled the room and clogged young Deron's lungs. He thought about breaking away and making a run for it. Ultimately, he decided against it since he knew that the percentage was pretty high that Paul would put a bullet in his back.

Deron stood there watching his mom who was obviously high on some drugs again. His dad was obviously drunk on that grown people drink again. Deron wondered if there was more to life. As soon as he was sure it was, he thought of his Janiya. Deron thought that he had to be in love since Janiya was on his mine while having a gun pointed at him. He also thought about Lorretta, and how he wanted to dart out of there to jump back in the back seat of her car.

Janiya crossed his mind more and more while the police officer begged his father to put the gun. Gloria still stood there fixing her clothes. There was something was wrong with her and it wasn't a pretty sight to Deron. He could see every bone in his mom's face and her eyes were beginning to bulge out of her eye sockets. Her clothes begged her to stop pulling, and if they could talk, they would tell her "I'm sorry, but we just don't fit." Her hair was full of sweat and blood. Dampened strands stuck to her angular face. Blood and bruises found a home on her arms. The belt she wore to hold the pants around her increasingly decreasing frame, felt out of place.

While Deron was stood there watching his mom, he was snatched from behind by a police officer and everything started to happen in slow motion.

Paul was staring at Gloria, Gloria screaming as she watched Deron being carried away. The police officer was staring at Paul and Deron was screaming and flailing his arms.

Two gunshots rang through his ears and blood soared through the soiled apartment. Deron tried to break away from the officer's arms, but to no avail. Gloria was thrown into the wall by the bullets from Paul's gun. As quick as she hit the wall, she hit the floor even quicker.

Deron finally was able to break free from the officer when he saw the bullets pierce through his mom's bloody chest. He managed to fight his way passed the other police officer's to run up to his mom. He bypassed Paul, who was shot in the head by the other officer. Gloria was desperately struggling to get some oxygen. Deron saw more officers and paramedics rush in.

He had a lot of anger and pain in his heart for Gloria, but tears showered from his eyes. Seeing his mom laying there with blood spilling from her body, made him feel a sense of sadness in his heart.

She laid there motionless and it was a different kind of motionless. Deron would sometimes closely watch her breathing whenever she was passed out from drugs or alcohol. He closely watched her again and he knew something was different.

"Baby?" Gloria said while gasping for breath. Kneeling down right beside her, Deron held her hand while also wiping tears away from her eyes.

"Yes momma, get up mom, come on."

"Baby?"

"Come on momma, you have to get up." Deron begged. He wasn't sure why, but the scene from Lion King popped in his head. When Mufasa fell into the herd of wilder beast, killing him and Simba tried his best to wake his dad. That's how he felt trying his best to get his mom up. Deron remained in denial of the current circumstances. She was dying and he knew it, but refused to accept it.

"Baby?"

"Yes momma." Deron sniffed.

"Remember that talk I had with you?"

"Yes I remember, if I say I'm gonna do something, make sure I do it. If I love something, make sure I love it whole heartedly. Yes momma, I remember and I will never forget."

"Good baby. Momma did something good then." Gloria said with a cough after each word. Her eyes blinked slowly, like a rose pedal falling from a withering flower. Deron had nothing to say, he just continued to look at her breathe her last breaths in his now bloody hands.

"Baby?" Gloria coughed again.

"Yes momma, I'm still here."

"I'm sorry I wasn't a better mom for you." Deron became angry, but somehow found a way to keep it inside. He was angry because she knew what Deron needed from her. She knew how much Deron wanted it and yet she still didn't give it to him. She knew how much he wanted her to tell him she loved him and yet she did nothing about it. She knew she wasn't being a good mother and yet, did nothing about it…So Deron thought.

"I love you son." Gloria said as she died right there in his arms.

Deron always thought of his parents as some "Selfish son of bitches." This moment had convinced him that he was completely right in his feelings. His whole life, he wanted to hear his mom tell him she loved him. She finally did, but waited until her last breath to tell him. The least she could do, in Deron's mind, was stay alive five more seconds so she can hear him say it back. Deron was furious as he thought "The selfish son of bitch wanted to get right with God before she died."

Deron figured fixing a wrong right before she died would do the trick. He no longer cared as dropped her hand right there and finally accepted being escorted out by the police.

Deron actually couldn't wait to get outside so he could see Lorretta again and maybe she can take him somewhere. She was nowhere to be found. He had no idea what will happen next in his life. Both of his parents were dead he had no nearby relatives that he could go to.

CHAPTER 9
JANIYA

Waking up, all Janiya could think about was Deron and the night they had and how it ended. She had an empty feeling in her stomach and there was regret in her heart.

She was prepared to tell Deron everything, but she didn't want to bring the night down with the drama she'd been dealing with. She was at peace when Deron swathed his arms around her slender frame. Janiya finally felt wanted and finally felt unconditionally loved. She felt something that she hadn't before. Love. Genuine Love.

Janiya has always known it to exist, but she's always wanted to know what it felt like. The thought of the feeling Deron gave her yesterday, made her heart smile, it made her have goose bumps. Overall, it sent chills throughout her body and numbing tingle enveloped her.

Deron was definitely starting to rub off on her because she found herself speaking with more passion and thinking more about her feelings. He was such a poet at heart and every word that came out of his mouth seemed to make her feel a certain way. The closest thing it could relate it to was how she felt about Lorretta, Just in a different way because, well, she liked Deron.

A part of her really appreciated Lorretta, but also questioned whether or not it was truly genuine because her dad paid her very well. With Deron, she knew that everything she got from him was genuine. She didn't care if it was only his friendship, although, she wanted more.

Janiya sat there in her bed going over those thoughts while looking out of her window.

"Baby, are you up?" Edna screamed from the other side of the door. A part of Janiya desperately wanted to ignore her, but she knew doing that would make her enter anyway.

"Yes Mother, I'm up." Janiya said while sitting up with her arms wrapped around her legs. Her head rested on her knees. She watched raindrops fill her window pane in hopes of a miracle return of Deron appearing on the other side.

"Ok, well get out of bed and put some clothes on. Your father has a very important meeting to attend and we are invited."

"Ok mother!" Janiya yelled.

"Janiya, you get out of the bed right now young lady!" Edna said as she barged into Janiya's room. She was already dressed to perfection.

Janiya always thought of her mom as a stunning woman, but also felt the beautiful gene eluded her. Her hair was perfect and often reminded her of the fancy spiral stairs that was in the richer people homes, her curls were amazing. Since she didn't have a job, she had plenty of time to work out and keep her body in perfect shape.

"Don't just sit there looking at me like that Janiya, we really have to get going."

"Where is Lorretta, she's normally the one that help me anyway?" Janiya said snapping back at her mother. She knew

Edna didn't have the time to sit there and go back and forth with her.

She hardly acknowledged Janiya and she was sure that some psychologist would say that it was an outcry for attention. Not that she cared anyway, all her mom cared about was Phillip and the money he made.

"Trust me Janiya, I'm looking for her as well, but she has yet to come in and has yet to return my calls. Just hurry up and get ready please." Edna said as she walked out, slamming Janiya's door shut.

Janiya was stuck in a huge, gigantic house around rich, and snotty people. Edna forced Janiya to be there knowing there wouldn't be any kids that would keep her company. Not that Janiya would talk to them anyway because the only person she really felt like talking to was Deron.

She hadn't seen him since last night and it was really killing her because she wished she could see him every single day. He and Lorretta both seemed to make life easy for Janiya.

Just the thought of Deron's face made her smile. The thought of hearing his voice, seeing his walk, made her forget about everything that was going on around her.

There were hundreds of people at the event casually walking, dancing and playing games. Somme meeting, Janiya thought as watched them all in anger. She didn't want to be there and it was evident. She found an unoccupied bench overlooking a huge lake that she made her spot to have alone.

Janiya turned to see her mother enjoying herself with all of the other rich housewives. They were all drinking something colorful and all had huge smiles painted on their faces.

Phillip was his normal self, looking as if he was kissing some major butt. Janiya's eyes quickly became filled with rage for what he had done to her a few nights ago. As if she needed something else to feel down about, now she had to deal with what he did to her and what he'd taken from her. Phillip obviously knew what he was doing by sending Edna to the store that night. Janiya came to conclusion that he had to have already planned it out ahead of time.

Slowly, images and moments from that day started to enter her mind and she became more and more angry at Phillip. This was the same man that claimed he loved her and her mother.

This was supposed to be her father, albeit, step father. He was supposed to be the one that protected her. She felt more protection when she was in the presence of Deron than around own father.

Again, Janiya became so angry that she actually thought about telling her mother everything that happened that rainy night when she sent him to the store.

She wanted her to know how he came into her room and threw himself on her, and inside her. Janiya wanted her to know the pain that she felt and the pain she continued to feel that very moment, physically and mentally.

Tears appeared and just continued to live in her eyes as she sat there watching the ripples in the lake with the sun beaming down on her. At that moment, Janiya's mind was made up. S knew what she was going to do and didn't care about who all knew and how bad it made their family look.

Janiya cleared the tears from the wells of her eyes. She repositioned some lose strands of hair and was on her way toward Edna.

It seemed her heartbeat and every step she took made a sound while walking. That sound got louder as Janiya saw Phillip's face. She saw mother excuse herself from the table while she took a call, but that wouldn't stop her as she was focused on finally getting something off of her chest.

"Mother?" Janiya said as she tugged at her red and white flower dress. Janiya was ignored with Edna being on the phone.

"What! Hold on one second please. Janiya, what is it? You see I am on the phone. Wait until I am off the phone please!"

"But mother, I need to tell you something."

"Janiya, I am on the phone. Ok, what were you saying sir?" Edna said, going back to her call. Janiya continued to tug away and Edna continued to do what she kept doing, changing directions and not listening to her.

"Phillip....Phillip... Phillip! Honey I need to tell you something!" Edna screamed, running in the direction of Phillip.

"But mother, I have to tell you something and it's important."

Edna kept the phone in her hand while she ran over to Phillip and Janiya stayed attached to her. She was determined to tell her what Phillip had done to her.

"Phillip baby?"

"Edna, baby what's wrong?" Phillip asked, holding his arms out. Janiya was amazed as she saw the act he was putting on in front of his people. Phillip seemed like he really cared what was going on with Edna. Maybe he was worried; maybe Janiya wasn't giving him any credit because of what he did to her.

At this point, Janiya couldn't care less if Phillip all of sudden turned into Jesus. He was just a different man when it came to caring for her mom today. She tried her best to keep the hatred that she had for him painted on her face. She wanted the anger remain in her heart.

"Edna, baby what's wrong? You're scaring me here, have a seat. Drink this, calm down and tell me what's going on."

Tears escaped Edna's eyes and screams sounded off from her mouth. Her hands covered her face while Phillip tried in vain to figure out what was going on with her.

"Edna!" Phillip screamed.

"Lorretta...Lorretta....Lorretta!" Edna screamed Lorretta's name several times while Phillip and others crowded themselves around her.

"What about Lorretta?" Phillip knelt down beside Edna. Janiya saw a thick piece of lumber wood lying under the bench she sat at earlier. She wondered how much trouble could she, or would she get in if she got it and launched it in the direction of Phillip's face.

It was a nice get away for her mind and it brought a smile to her face, but it quickly went away when she started to wonder what happened to Lorretta.

Before she knew it, she was headed on her way to Edna again and this time out of fear, not anger.

"Edna, talk to me, what happened to Lorretta?"

"Phillip honey, she's gone. Lorretta, she's gone.....she's gone!"

"Who was that on the phone Edna? I need you to tell me what's going on here. What happened to Lorretta?" Phillip and his friends tried their best to get Edna to calm down, but obviously something terrible happened to Lorretta.

"Mother, what happened to Lorretta?" Janiya asked and surprisingly to her, she was the only one who was able to get a reaction out of Edna. Her arms were thrown around Janiya in the most genuine hug that she had ever received. Instantaneously, tears fell and it was such an overflowing stream of pain.

Edna and Janiya there crying, hugging for two totally different reasons. Edna because of what happened to Lorretta and for Janiya, it was because she felt what it was like to have a mother.

A huge part of Janiya wanted so badly to selfishly remain embracing her mother, but another part of her felt the need to really find out what happened to Lorretta. Still enclosed around each other, tears continued to fall from their eyes. Janiya spotted Phillip out of the corner of her tear filled eyes. If minds could speak to each other, then Janiya would be in trouble for saying words that she was not allowed to say.

Janiya didn't understand a lot of things about life, but there were definitely a few things she did know. She knew that she hated Phillip with a burning passion. She was getting to the point where she really wanted him to know how much she despised and hated him. Janiya felt he took her mother away from her years ago after her real father died. Phillip and Edna told her that he was killed by a drunk driver. Phillip at the time was the police officer that came to their house that rainy night. Although Janiya was young, she hated him then just as much as she does now, well even more.

"Mother, what happened to Lorretta?" Janiya finally ask after sitting there with Edna while people continued to pat us on their backs as they cried their hearts out.

"Baby, Lorretta is dead. She died in Oak Cliff last night from a drunk driver. What was she even doing in Oak Cliff?" Edna cried out as she asked questions to no one.

Janiya sat there, still as a tree stump. Only one thing, one person entered her mind. Janiya was devastated over what happened to Lorretta. She really didn't know what else to feel because the only person that entered her mind was Deron.

Was Deron with Lorretta? Was Deron dead also? She felt like a horrible person and in her head, she apologized to God and to Lorretta. Janiya said that she was sorry for thinking of someone else when Lorretta was the one that died.

She was confused and lost. All of the anger that she had before, came back. The rage that Janiya had inside when she walked up to Edna initially, came back.

Janiya let go of her mother, stood up and looked Phillip dead in the eye with pure rage. If hearts could cry, not of sadness, but of anger, then her heart was creating oceans that wanted Phillip drown horribly.

Hundreds of people at this business gathering all had their eyes painted on Phillip because of the glare Janiya was giving him.

Edna was left hugging a chair in pure agony over the sudden bad news surrounding Lorretta. There was a plethora of pain, hurt and anger that Janiya had burning inside her.

Lorretta was dead, and Janiya had no clue if Deron was also dead. Edna was a wreck and Phillip raped her. Those were the obvious details Janiya had to succumb to.

If Phillip hadn't raped Janiya, she never would have been as distant with Deron and he wouldn't have felt the need to come to her house late at night. Lorretta never would have had to take Deron home and she would still be here. Edna wouldn't be sitting there crying her heart out. It was clear who Janiya blamed for all of this.

Suddenly, she felt her eyes piercing in the direction of Phillip. Her teeth seemed to clinch and the left corner of her mouth began to resemble a pit bull mouth when he sought out something he wanted to attack. She wanted Phillip, she wanted blood, and she wanted to attack him. For the first time, words entered her mind that she never knew would ever enter. Janiya wanted to kill Phillip.

CHAPTER 10

1994 Deron 18

It's been about 3 years since Deron seen the gorgeous Janiya. Not one single day has passed where he didn't think about her. He craved the scent of her presence, like rose petals that bloomed in a mid day rain.

Her energy and her smile always seemed to remind him of the happiest dandelion that smiled bright in the summer's breeze. She was his water, air, and his everything. Deron missed her more than anything.

During the three years that Deron hadn't seen Janiya, he began writing out his thoughts more and more. He sat at his desk and pulled out his notebook and began to write.

There was a sense of panic in the air and trouble high in the clouds. Embers burned from yesterday's fires. A lost love buried beneath the rubble, but still there's life, still there's love, still there was a want to go on, a need to keep going. I desperately look forward to the days where there would be less panic in the air. The clouds would suddenly disappear. The rain would still escape the sky and fall upon my heart where she used to be and the thunderstorms would become my heartbeat. Lightning would become my fuel, my adrenaline to keep searching and to continue loving the thought of love. I would continue dreaming about Janiya until she came true. The sense of panic would have escaped the air, clouds and rain would be an afterthought and the only embers that burned would be the fire that I had for her. The passion I provided when I dreamed Janiya into existence would send us both whirling in loves' ecstasy. It was at that point when I realized that I was definitely, definitely, in love and for reasons only Janiya would understand, I smiled.

"Deron honey, your food is ready!" Deron's foster mother, Ms. Sylvie, yelled up to his room.

"Ok Ms. Sylvie, I'll be right down!"

"Deron honey, how many times must I tell you? Call me Sylvie or mother like the rest of the kids." Ms. Sylvie said as Deron imagined her strong high cheekbones.

A lot has happened since that tragic night 3 years ago when Gloria and Paul died. Deron bounced around from 3 different foster homes and was currently on his 4th now. The first set of parents was ok, not too different from the lifestyle he had with his own parents. Mr. and Mrs. Tidewell were good people, but lived in a bad area just as Deron did and he ran into the same guys that tried him before. They soon found out that trying him was a waste of time because Deron really had nothing to live for, so therefore, had nothing to lose.

Deron believed the Tidewell's grew frustrated with him because all he wanted to do was run away and seek out Janiya.

Some nights, he simply refused to go home and would rather find an abandoned car somewhere to fall asleep. That was until some cops found him and returned him back to the Tidewell's. They requested that Deron returned to the system, because they did not want to deal with him anymore.

Then there were the Johnson's and the Ogdenhurst's. They were both older white couples which were fooled from the start. The foster care presented Deron perfectly; they cleaned him up, gave him a nice haircut and taught him how to speak eloquently.

They put Deron in a rented suit and tie and basically told him how to fool people in interviews. Also, it didn't hurt that they smudged his background a bit when interested couples would inquire about him.

Deron almost began quoting their spill for them. He had it memorized in his brain. 'Deron Jamison is one of, if not the most intelligent young men we have. He was an inner city kid that kept his head buried in books and never got involved in gangs or drugs. Deron has read over 100 books since being here and has also started writing poetry.'

There was more mumbo jumbo that spilled out of their mouths and those poor white people took the bait. Soon after Deron was with them, he became the kid with all of the potential in the world and would go on to do great things, but wasn't quite a good fit.

It was fine with Deron, because in the end, he was matched with a great person, Ms. Sylvie. She was a 57 year old French lady that took in foster kids and she shared a passion for writing as did Deron. Her house was an old ranch style home. Fairly aged wood floors and wood paneling dressed her home favorably. Greenery was strategically placed throughout and hundreds of photos were plastered against the walls.

It took Deron some time to figure out if Ms. Sylvie gave him attention because she really did like him or if she sympathized with him. Either way, Deron was fine with it. He just wanted to know which one he was dealing with so he knew what and what not to expect. Deron absolutely hated not knowing something.

"Deron your food is getting cold baby boy." Ms. Sylvie said yelling up to the sluggish Deron. He loved to hear her accent and instantly made him think of Lorretta.

"Coming Ms. Sylvie!" Deron yelled. He felt the corners of her mouth frown up and could see her eyes angling in frustration at him.

"Deron, its Sylvie or mother!" Ms. Sylvie said, pointing her finger at Deron while he dashed down the squeaky wooden steps.

Deron sat at the squeaky clean glass table with outdated table mates. He loved Ms. Sylvie's cooking and couldn't wait to dig in.

Home cooked meals were not out of the ordinary in the Sylvie home and Deron loved that. He said grace along with the 3 other kids, Julia age 15, Alex 16, and Vanessa 17.

Deron became very fond of Vanessa; she was the one girl that gave him different feelings in one special area. No one has ever measured up to flawless Janiya, but Vanessa was stunning and she was available to Deron, unlike Janiya.

She sat at the table looking at Deron with the most tempting hazel eyes that he'd ever seen. She wore her hair in natural curls and he was a sucker for her purple hue, her purple tone. Vanessa was a luscious dark skinned girl and Deron loved to sit and watch her.

All of the kids had their own issues and insecurities that they dealt with. Vanessa had been in the system for 8 years now after Child Protective Services took her away. Her mom had been arrested numerous times for prostitution. She also ran away hundreds of times before coming to Ms. Sylvie.

Julia, a thick Puerto Rican that was very talkative, sensed Deron's infatuation with Vanessa and she tried in vain to stray his attention away from her. She planted bad information about Vanessa in Deron's head, but it was to no avail because he had his mind made up of wanting Vanessa.

Julia said that Vanessa's mom was a "Famous Prostitute" Deron wondered how someone could be a "Famous Prostitute" He often ignored Julia and the weird comments she made about Vanessa.

What Julia didn't know, was that Deron wasn't easily convinced, strayed or pressured into a judgment of someone if he didn't feel it himself.

The word around the foster home was that Vanessa's mom had been on T.V plenty of times. Also, it was said that she slept with hundreds of famous people that for some reason felt the need to have the company of a prostitute.

Vanessa often paid the price for her mom choosing the occupation that she chose. Many guys tried to hit on and sleep with her. They believed Vanessa would follow in her mom's footsteps, but she was nothing like that.

While Deron salivated over the beauty of Vanessa, Ms. Sylvie asked him something that she normally asked in privacy.

"Deron honey?"

"Yes Ms. Sylvie?" Deron said hesitantly. She glared at Deron with her head down. Her thin glasses rested on the tip of her nose while her eyes pierced at Deron.

"Deron, I guess I will just have to start telling you to call me Ms. Sylvie so you can start calling me something else. Kid, why must you always do the opposite of what I ask of you? Anyway, tell us something nice Deron."

Ms. Sylvie always asked Deron to tell her something nice and that was her way of getting him to share some poetry. Sometimes he would freestyle, but most times, he would share something he had memorized. He always tried to pretend like he didn't hear her, but figured he was happy to since Vanessa was sitting there ready to listen.

"Ok Ms. Sylvie, I can do that for you. Do you have special requests?" Deron calmly and confidently asked. He was a nervous wreck inside because he wanted so badly to impress Vanessa.

Deron glanced over at Vanessa and she was a million miles away, and that disappointed him. She hovered over her plate while her head rested against her hand. Her elbows were cemented to the table.

Alex was always listening to his walkman, distancing himself. Deron felt he did so to let everyone know that he couldn't care less about what was going on. Julia sat there quietly, eating her food, yet very interested in what Deron was about to say. A smile was drawn over her face. Once Deron looked in her direction, she couldn't have shown more of her braces. She was beyond excited. Deron scanned the room once again and laid eyes on Ms. Sylvie, she waved her hands out as if she was saying "Well, come on with it."

"Ok ok ok Ms. Sylvie, here goes." Deron cleared his throat.

I'm in love with tasting raindrops. Especially the drops that found resting places along her windows. I like to make it rain, so I could see my baby's raindrops land and create streaks as they fall into my dehydrated opening. Making for a thirsty puddle of creamy decadence. I love to make it thunderstorm so I could lie excitingly beneath her beautiful sky. I would catch mouthfuls at a time, hoping to quench my thirst. Mmmmmm I love to grab her clouds and hold them tight. My begging organ that resided in my mouth was getting impatient. Finally, it erected toward her heavens and twirled twister like inside her erotic, tasty atmosphere. I kept the rain coming. After her storm, raindrops clung enjoyably from the place she loved to be the most, the place she loved seeing raindrops..... my wood, her home. The sun was setting in the horizon, the leaves in the trees breezed like the elevated pastures in the motherlands. In the lonely distance, chirped playful baby birds. Gorgeous butterflies pranced and danced and it was there a beautiful woman with curly hair stood. Her hair was tied in a ponytail and being held with one hand so she could enjoy removing the raindrops that resided on her home, my wood. Have you tasted your lover's raindrops?

Deron was done and the look on Ms. Sylvie's was priceless. Her eyes didn't move and her shoulders were drawn back. She dabbed the corners of her mouth with her napkin and looked around. Alex still bobbed his head to the beat of the music and Julia still sat there finishing off her meal and gazing at Deron. Vanessa raised her head, sucked her teeth and sighed.

"Something you want to say Vanessa?" Ms. Sylvie said while sitting back in her chair.

"Well mother, I just would like to know is that all Deron knows to talk about?" Vanessa said while still having her head buried in her plate. She stabbed the peas one by one before shoving them in her mouth.

"Vanessa, as you know, since you have been here the longest of the children that are here, I believe in expressing yourself however you see fit and if this is what was inside Deron's mind, then he is allowed to express it. It was a little too erotic in my opinion, but the way he used his words and expressed himself, opening himself up and the way he delivered his words were great. I'm sure there was a reason Deron chose the subject he chose, maybe he saw something on T.V., or maybe there's just something or someone in his heart that he misses. Maybe there's someone that he's seen recently. Is there anything you would like to share Vanessa?" Ms. Sylvie asked while quickly becoming Deron's best friend.

Vanessa rolled her eyes and pushed herself away from the table and walked away. Deron recognized a familiar feeling that he had once before and he wasn't sure how to process it. It was the same feeling he had with Janiya. Any time her heart was hurt, his heart was hurt.

He saw the pain in Vanessa's walk and wanted to fix her. Deron quickly stood and requested that Vanessa stop to listen to he had to say. She did so, but kept her back turned to him as she fiddled with her hands. Her weight was shifted from one side of well-formed body, to the other.

Last night I had 2 angels show up in my bedroom. Each with smiles painted on their faces. One spoke while the other sat and smiled. "It's ok baby, granny is doing great. I'm in no more pain as you can see. Look, I can even dance. Praise Jesus." My father's mom said as she raised her no longer wrinkled hand. She was so famous for doing that and I often imitated her. "Baby?" She said and I smiled because I just loved when she started off her statements and speeches that way. "Baby, thank you for the lovely words you spoke at granny's homegoing. Now I never cried a lot, but let's just say baby, you made one of God's angels shed joyful and proud tears. Granny always knew you were special and had a gift even when you thought I was being hard on you. Let everyone know that granny is fine. I love you baby." She held onto my hand and smiled at me. She watched as tears attempted to come rushing out and smiled one last time while going to sit at edge of my bed. Now my grandmother, my mother's mom, whom I haven't seen since I was 9, gave me a hug. She knelt down beside me with that huge smile she had. "Deron, look at you. Oh my world!" She says. I guess she's been up there listening to my mom say that "oh my world!" I smiled. "Look at you. You have turned into a very handsome man, look at you. You are amazing and you will do great things in this world, you hear me?" She asked. She was simply beautiful and I couldn't believe how stunning she was. I mean she looked just like I remember, curly hair, round angelic face , deep eyes that you could just fall in and would have felt like heaven. Her touch was just as powerful. Strong, yet soft. "Now Deron, I need you to do something for me. Stay exactly who you are, no matter what. People will attempt to steal your joy, don't you dare let them. Another thing, I need you to kiss your momma for me. Let her know to enjoy life, because it can be taken from you very quick. Let her know that I am happy, I am fine. I love you Deron! Always remember that." Both, my Granny and Grandmother stood over me, placing their hands over me and together closing my eyes. Needless to say, I slept peacefully from the visits of my 2 angels!

"So to answer your question Vanessa, sex is not all I know. I'm able to speak about things I haven't experienced personally. It's my way living out my thoughts or releasing some pain that I've seen others experience. This story was made up Vanessa. I create family members because mine were so jacked up. I've never known any of my grandparents and my parents are dead, so I create family to help me cope with the loneliness that I feel. Ms. Sylvie said my words were erotic, and be that it may, but I don't have a family, I don't have love, I don't have anything. I do have my mind and my mind allows me to have the things I've always desired." Deron said as he scanned around the room.

Vanessa heard Deron out, but never turned to face him. She continued to mess around with her fingers and when he finished his speech, she slow stepped her way up the stairs. Vanessa stopped midway to give Deron a mysterious look and then she disappeared.

"Deron, that was beautiful, just simply beautiful." Ms. Sylvie said. She used the same napkin that she used to dab the corners of her mouth to wipe the tears away that Deron brought on.

"Deron, you have such a special way with words and I just love hearing what you have to say and yes, even the erotic stuff." Ms. Sylvie chuckled and sniffed at the same time, still wiping the tears that escaped her eyes.

Deron gave Ms. Sylvie a nod that let her know he appreciated the kind words and he slowly sat down, finishing off his dinner while the other kids left.

After Ms. Sylvie removed herself from the table, Deron was the only one left there and he began to think about how much he was beginning to really like Vanessa.

Sadly, Vanessa was Deron's weird amazing, deadly cancer. He was in love with someone that he shouldn't love. He felt that he should be waiting for his incredible Janiya to prance aggressively, yet gracefully into his life.

Who was he kidding, it's been 3 years since their eyes last spoke to each other, 3 years since their lips last craved each other's. Deron asked himself if it would be ok for him to tackle loves chemotherapy and enjoy the fruitful love of the amazing Vanessa.

Although it's been 3 years, his heart still talked to Janiya's heart. Although it's been 3 years, his mind still made love to Janiya's mind. Although it's been 3 years, he was still in love with the beautiful Janiya, but what would he do about Vanessa? Deron's thoughts clashed.

He sat there at the table with a confused heart, because he was starting to think of Vanessa they way he thought Janiya. He wanted to protect her like he protected Janiya. He wanted to touch her heart the same way he wanted to touch Janiya's heart.

He even started paying more attention to Vanessa, way more than he could admit with Janiya.

Vanessa had a fondness for roses and he had a habit of wanting to know more about whatever made women happy. In this case with Vanessa, since she loved roses, every inch of a rose was his focus.

When he first crossed paths with her, she seemed very much like Deron. She was a withered rose that people would love to help bring back to life, but often left that job to someone else.

Although a withered rose was the way she came off, it was nowhere near the way Deron saw her. She was his coral rose and he desired every inch of her body. A body that made the stem of his love maker rise to the heavens. He desired her heart ferociously, hoping the day would come that her love petals would bloom and blossom. It would leave no prickles, or thorns, on the stem of his heart.

Vanessa and Deron were friends above all, but he truly believed she wanted to be rescued by him and he was very much obliged at the attempt of such a feat. The more they confided to each other about their past, the more Vanessa became his red tipped yellow rose. If only she knew that she was the one doing the rescuing, then hopefully, the raindrops that rested upon the petals of her heart, would be those of passion and love.

She was a friend that Deron had fallen in love with and for the moment, all powers of rescuing Vanessa had become nonexistent. Only for a moment because it was his goal to not be what others were to him and Vanessa.

Deron wouldn't walk by the withered rose that needed to be brought back to life. She would reside in the sunny world of his garden, and he would fertilize her with all of the love he could. In hopes she would sprout gracefully from the dead withered rose that she thought of herself as and into the beautiful red rose. The red rose that he saw her as from the moment he laid eyes on her freshly bloomed petals.

It was his goal to make her feel that she was a blooming and vibrant rose again. As soon as he thought he had it figured out, his heart began to break because it meant the coming to a realization that Janiya may be no more and that hurt like hell.

CHAPTER 11

1994 Janiya 17

For the third consecutive year Janiya was left waiting to see if Deron would show up for school. As she walked through the doors of Thomas Jefferson High School for her senior year, she knew she wouldn't see him, but Janiya kept that wish alive because she didn't want to believe what was in her heart.

The only news that came out about Lorretta's accident was that it was caused by a drunk driver. There was nothing further about if Deron was with her or not. Deron's 3 year silence had just about convinced Janiya that he was indeed with Lorretta that night. She knew how Deron operated, and going that long without hearing from him wasn't the way.

If she could see Deron or talk to him, she would let him know how much she missed him and how much she needed him right now, even if it was just as friends.

Janiya fought with herself for not telling Deron what was going on with her, and for not telling him what Phillip was doing to her and continued to do. She recalled that night very well and she remembered how close she came to telling Deron everything. She forced herself to believe that if Lorretta hadn't come into her room, then she would have eventually told Deron everything.

Over the last few years, Janiya slowly began to hate the only woman that genuinely cared about her and even that made her sad, but she couldn't help what was in her heart. Deron was her everything and as she sat down in the cold cafeteria, the corners of her full pouty lips began to turn up and her eyes seemed to gaze as she reminisced of her days when she would watch Deron on the dusty playground.

Janiya always felt Deron looking at her and it made her feel weird at first, nervous almost. She would break out into a salty sweat, leaving her drenched when she returned back to class. Her face would become flushed with embarrassment and eagerness that he would one day stare at her long enough until she looked back. Janiya always tried not to look at him or at least not let him see her looking at him, because she didn't know what he thought of her at the time and she didn't want to come off as the weird girl.

"Girl is that you?" A girl screamed, interrupting Janiya's thought of Deron.

"That is you J, J hey girl!" It was Layla, and she was more beautiful than Janiya remembered. The years had really been good to her. She couldn't believe how beautiful Layla had become.

She was blessed with a nicely, blossomed pair of breast that Janiya had been praying for. Her hair was different, still dark, but it was short with big curly locks. They lost contact around the same time Deron and Janiya did. Her dad took a job in California, but they were back, and for Janiya, it was great to see a familiar face.

"Layla, is that you?" Janiya screamed while hopping out of her seat, knowing it was her.

"Hey girl, how have you been? Your favorite color is still purple I see." Layla stated as they embraced each other. "Yes, purple is still my favorite color, but anyway when did you get back in Texas? I'm so glad to see you girl, you look great."

Janiya couldn't stop herself from looking over Layla and loving her look. She still looked like Chili from TLC, if not better with the perky new addition on her chest. Her skin was flawless and she started wearing makeup, which brought back Janiya's jealous feelings of Layla.

Her eyes were a deep brown and seemed to always have a twinkle to them. Layla had always been gorgeous to Janiya and all of the boys always liked her. Janiya didn't blame them.

"Yea girl, we're back in Texas. My dad missed playing golf with your dad, I guess. I was hoping I would see you at school this year.

"Stepdad! He's my stepdad, in fact, just call him Phillip!" Janiya snapped.

Her eyes filled with rage, like a volcano boiling with lava, and the thought of hearing Phillip being her dad just made Janiya want to erupt. Janiya stood there, motionless, with her hands drawn back, lips curled up and nose turned up like she smelled something horrible.
"Ok....girl...Phillip." Janiya and Layla both sat at the table with an awkward silence hanging around like an unwanted guest.

The bell finally ended the awkwardness and both girls stood, grabbing their backpacks and throwing them over one shoulder. Janiya pulled her long crimped hair in front of her so that it rested upon her chest.

"Well ok girl, I hope I see you later. Do you still stay in the same house? If so, you can ride home with me. I heard about Lorretta and I never got to talk you about it." Layla said as they walked in the same direction to their class.

"Yea L, we're still in the same house, but it's ok. Maybe we can ride together another day."

"Ok girl, I forgot all about L and J. I can't believe you remembered we use to call each other that." Layla said as she laughed while nudging Janiya with her boney elbow.

Janiya remembered how much she hated Layla, but it was mostly out of jealousy. It was also the horrible way Layla treated Deron.

Deron was beneath Layla and he wasn't allowed to speak, look, walk, or think anything Layla's way. You would think since Layla and Janiya shared the same rich girl status, they would think the same about Deron. Janiya was able to see the inside of Deron and see parts of him others neglected.

"Yea L, I remembered and don't worry about not being able to talk to me about Lorretta, I'm sure we'll have plenty of things to talk about now with you being back in Texas."

"Ok J, well I'm gonna get to class." Layla said, but before Janiya left, she stopped her for one last question.

"L! Wait! Real quick, do you remember that kid Deron?" Janiya asked with her hazel eyes, just as big as the moon.

"Girl! You mean that homeless boy? J, last I heard he's somewhere in a foster home now. His crazy parents killed each other and as a matter of fact, I think it happened the same night that Lorretta died."

Janiya tried in vain to hide her smile, but as she stood there listening to Layla talk, the only thing she focused on was Deron not being dead. She started thinking things that she hadn't thought before.

She instantly thought about hearing Deron's voice and him whispering in her ear. Janiya imagined her eyes being closed as Deron entered inside her while making both of her knees buckle simultaneously. He would touch her with the tips of his fingers while breathing erotic breaths into her ear. It would leave Janiya gasping and panting for breath.

Janiya's pinky finger started to make its way to the corner of her mouth and her eyes seemed to wander off in space while still listening to Layla go on and on about why she was even thinking about Deron.

Janiya's mind stayed in dreamland as she visualized his hand lifting her chin to taste her caramel flesh. She reacted by melting into his hand and tossing out orgasmic moans.

Janiya would open her eyes only to realize that Deron never physically touched her. That's how Deron would make her feel when he whispered the words "I love you" to her. Janiya just experienced a true mental orgasm while standing there twirling her hair.

"J! J!" Layla screamed while snapping her fingers in front of Janiya's eyes.

"Yea, what is it?" Janiya replied, finally coming back to reality.

"Girl, what happened to you? I said why you even thinking about him and stop smiling like that. Did you even hear that I said that the boys' parents were killed?"

Just like that, Janiya's fantasy was over and she started thinking about everything Deron had to deal with and she knew he had no one to talk to.

"Girl, we will talk later because you already late to class." Layla said as she walked away shaking her head. Janiya walked away feeling bittersweet. Her head and eyes drooped to the ground like armor being thrown into the ocean, sinking slowly, but surely.

"Hey baby, how was your first day of school?" Janiya's mother asked with a huge smile on her face. Janiya figured her mom wanted her to share some good news, but after the news she got about Deron, she couldn't think of anything that would satisfy Edna.

"It was fine mother, nothing spectacular happened. Oh, Layla and her family are back in Texas and I saw her today at school."

"Oh baby, that's great! Now you don't have to find a new best friend, and maybe she can help you get out of whatever funk you've been in for these last few years. I tell ya honey, I don't know if it's me, you, or what happened to Lorretta, but you seem to not care about looking good like any other normal girl at your age would." Edna said while fixing Phillip something to eat.

Edna diced the onions and wore an apron that said "Kiss The Cook." She shook her head while striding over to the sink.

Janiya stood there with her hand on her hips thinking 'did this lady really come out and say that.' Janiya rolled her eyes and shifted her weight to her other leg. She so badly wanted to say "Maybe it's because your fucking husband is raping me, have you ever thought about that?" On cue, Phillip walked in tossing his briefcase on the counter and loosening his tie. He glanced over at Janiya before kissing Edna on the cheek.

"Hi honey, dinner will be ready shortly." Edna said as she kissed Phillip and wiped her sticky red lipstick from his lips. After seeing that gross exchange, Janiya rolled her eyes once again and headed to her room, but only to be stopped.

"Hey baby girl, how was your first day of high school? Did anything special happen today and what classes do you have?" Phillip asked, completely fooling Edna with his interest in what was going on with Janiya. She stood there with her back still turned away from her mother and step father.

"Honey, don't be rude! You hear your father talking to you.....Well....do you?"

"Yes mother, I do." Janiya said while never making contact. Her eyes stayed planted to the cold black and white tiled kitchen floor.

"Well answer him right now young lady." Edna screamed while slamming the shiny overused knife down on the counter.

"Well step father, I had a great first day of senior year and I can't wait til' it's over so I can get out of this hell hole." Janiya screamed while staring in the raged eyes of Phillip.

"Janiya! What has gotten into you? You apologize to your father and go to your room, now!"

"It's ok baby." Phillip said as he waved at Edna, never taking his eyes off Janiya.

"It's ok baby. She will get was she has coming her way." Phillip said with a cynical look on his face. He stood tall and upright, popping his knuckles while he and Janiya had a stare down competition until Janiya broke the silence.

"What's wrong Philly boy? You scared to do it in front of my mother?" Janiya said as she walked toward Phillip while wrapping her hair up in a ball as if she was preparing herself for a battle. Phillip's eyes finally broke away from Janiya's eyes and he looked her up and down, wondering what she had planned.

"Janiya! Go to your room right now young lady! I don't know what happened to you at school, but whatever it was; it's no excuse to disobey your father. Now go to your room right now!" Edna said, glaring at Janiya with the same fiery eyes that Janiya stared at her step father.

"He is not my father! My father would never do to me the things that this man has!" Janiya said, finally getting fed up with Phillip being called her father.

She faced her mother as her lips trembled while desperately trying to keep from crying. Her eyes were red and watered as she walked toward Edna while looking at Phillip the entire time. Janiya stopped just a few feet in front of her mom and looked around the home that she never felt at home in. She saw the family photos, not one including her biological father, but she never questioned it. She saw everything about her father erased.

Phillip made sure that when they moved away from the home of Edna and Jason, there would be nothing to remember him of. There were all new pictures, all new furniture, even new plants and decorations, all new everything for the newly built family by Phillip.

"Mother?"

"Yes Janiya what is it? Why are you crying? You still need to apologize to your father." Edna said as she pointed in Phillip's direction. Phillip sat at the edge of the old wooden antique bar stool, rubbing the stubble on his face. His five o'clock shadow was getting worked over since he had no idea what Janiya was about to say.

"Mother, I have something to tell you. I probably should have told you a long time ago when it first happened, but...."

"But what honey? What is it? And why are you crying? Talk to me." Edna said as she wiped her hands on her apron and then taking it off. To Janiya's surprise, Phillip was quiet. Janiya's face was a mess and her hair was that much worse. She kept her head down as if her mom's face was painted on her shoes.

"Janiya what is it?" Edna said as she placed her hands on Janiya's shoulders and frantically looking at Phillip.

"Mother, like I said, I should have told you this sooner. It all started about 3 years ago. Phillip sent you out to the store and...and..and he came into my room mother and...did some things to me." Edna covered her face with her hand

and slowly backed away from Janiya. The timer on the oven sounded and Phillip glanced over, only to ignore it and continue to listen to Janiya. There was not one worried crack painted on the face of Phillip, he sat there running his hands threw his thinning hair.

"Mother he sent you out and then came into my room. I was so scared and I didn't know what to do. He told me that if I told you, then he would kill us both. Mother, first this man touched me in places he shouldn't have touched and then he put his fingers inside me. Then after all of that mother, he forced himself inside me. I tried mother, I tried to get him off, but he forced himself on me and there was nothing I could do. Any chance he could get, he would rape me. It's a sad world mother when my father as you call him, took my virginity. He is not and never was a father of mine. I'm in love with someone mother and I can't help but feel that I'm not fit to be loved. So this funky mood you say I've been in for the last few years is because your husband has been raping me, leaving me feeling dirty and nasty, inside and out. Mother how could you not know what was going on with me? I'm 17 and I can barely have normal thoughts about sex, but each time I do, I get the image of what Phillip does to me in my head. Erasing those thoughts of Deron, yes Deron. They seem to be nonexistent now. You know what mother? I had a great thought today about a boy, it was about him making love to me, and for the first time, I felt normal. I felt needed and wanted by someone the normal way, not with someone taking something from me." Janiya stood there wiping the tears away from her face and her mom sat in a chair spaced out, taking it all in.

Phillip continued to sit in the wooden chair with his chin resting in his hand, waiting for Janiya's story to be over with.

Janiya walked over to Edna and knelt down before her, grabbing her hand and wiping her face again with her other hand. Not being able to look her daughter in the eye, Edna quickly turned her face away and stared out into the grassy backyard, wishing it was just another day.

She wished it was just another day where she would be laying outside in the hammock with Phillip, drinking wine and enjoying some great conversation. Today was definitely the complete opposite and instead of swinging, relaxing on the comfortable and soothing hammock, she's hearing her daughter tell her the awful news of being molested and raped by the man she chose to marry.

"Mother? Do you understand what I'm telling you here? Why aren't you looking at me, or talking to me mother?" Janiya cried out.

"Baby, I...I...I don't know what to say. I mean...I just don't know."

"Well, can you just look at me please? Do you believe me?" Janiya begged for an answer or at least a response.

"She believes you." Phillip said as Janiya saw his tall frame standing in front of his seat.

He slammed his hands inside the pockets of his gray slacks that he hasn't been able to get out of. The pitch black eyes of Phillip were angled and his right eye slightly twitched as he lit and puffed a cigarette. Phillip inched closer and closer to Janiya, sarcastically laughing while he sandwiched the cigarette between his two fingers.

"She believes you. Don't you honey?" Phillip said as he blew cigarette smoke in the direction of Edna. She sat there still gazing outside in the backyard with tears filling her eyes.

"No..No..No...No." Edna finally responded.

"Honey, yes you do, you might as well tell her now." Phillip said while taking a puff of his cigarette, still smiling.

"Mother what is he talking about?" Janiya sobbed as she grabbed her mother's chin away from her view of the backyard.

"Mother what is he talking about?" Janiya repeated.

"She knows, ok!"

"She knows what?" Janiya screamed in the face of Phillip while standing to her feet.

Her once cheerful and always joyous expressions left quickly and pain was evident on the face of Edna. Her eyes never once looked in the direction of Janiya. Her arms lie dead across her lap.

Tears had stained Edna's caramel skin and her lips shook uncontrollably. She kept shaking her head as if she was telling someone no and her face continued to frown up. Edna was in disbelief that this situation was happening to her family.

"What does my mother know?" Janiya demanded

"Edna baby, answer your daughter please! If you don't, I will gladly do it for you."

Edna's eyes slowly glanced toward Janiya and as they locked on her, tears flooded from Edna's eyes.

"Mother, what's wrong? Can you just tell me already?"

"I...I..I.." Edna stuttered and her hands were drawn out in front of her as if they were speaking for her.

"She knows what I've been doing to you Janiya! There, honey, now she knows. Finally she can stop feeling like she has this big secret about me, shit! Ya know, I never really liked your daughter and I've been hoping this day would come. Something else I want to tell you both. I'm leaving!" Phillip said while fixing himself something to drink. He walked away from Edna and Janiya like he had nothing to worry about, so bold, so confident.

"Wait! Phillip, wait! Don't go, please baby!" Edna stood up and chased Phillip, leaving Janiya standing next to the chair she pushed herself out of.

Janiya stared at the chair in denial about what just occurred. She just told her mother that her step father was molesting and raping her for the last few years and her mom knew the entire time.

Not only did Edna not say anything about it, but the only reaction from her came when Phillip threatened to leave and that hurt Janiya the most.

Janiya cried uncontrollably as she watched her mother in the living room. The sun beamed through the curtains and she saw her mother begging on bended knee for Phillip not to leave. Edna clutched around Phillips leg and he, the alpha male that he was, soaked it all up, never telling her to stop. Janiya ran upstairs to her room, packed her things and opened the door. Before walking out, she turned and looked at her mom and Phillip. As tears streamed down her face, she turned and walked out.

CHAPTER 12

Deron 18

Things had began to change at Ms. Sylvie's foster home and usually the old yet sweet French lady had strict rules about her foster children dating each other, but what she began to see was beyond her control. The now tall and increasingly handsome Deron would read to the captivating Vanessa and she started to love it more and more. Anything, any style of poetry she wanted, Deron had it for her whenever she wanted.

The 6'2, 185 pound, chiseled Deron worked at the City of Fort Worth Library stocking books after school and whenever he could read some poetry, he jumped at it. Poetry became another form, if not the best form of communication for Deron. It allowed him to use his imagination and escape different worlds and somehow bring worlds together whenever he wanted.

Deron wasn't the dirty and homeless kid around school that people remembered when he was younger. In fact, he had become pretty popular at Dennis G. Holman High School. He was involved in talent shows and school plays, sometimes even directing them. Vanessa was always there to root Deron on.

She fell for Deron because of his poetic and creative mind and the magnetic panache he had with people. He was the type that would help any and everyone out if he saw they needed it.

Vanessa loved that aspect of Deron's personality and the fact that the most handsome man to her carried himself like he was the most normal person around was a turn on to her.

They tried their best to sneak around Ms. Sylvie, but she knew what was going on and just let them feel like they were getting away with it. What Ms. Sylvie didn't know was that sometimes they snuck into each other's room for some late night pillow talk. The nights would be pitch black and Deron would wait until all of the lights were off and he knew Ms. Sylvie had a routine. She would shower, walk the dark hallway to put dirty towels in the hamper, slowly walk to the bathroom to spend another 15 minutes there before yawning on her way to her bedroom.

Deron had to be extra careful because all of the kid's bedrooms were upstairs. They had to be very cautious when sneaking into each other's bedrooms. Deron waited five minutes after Ms. Sylvie's old wooden door clapped shut. He would then wait five more minutes for Vanessa to turn on her light so Deron could see it beneath the door. That was his cue that she was ready for him.

This particular night was going according to plan. Ms. Sylvie had her hair wrapped up and had on a long blue and white flowered gown with white house shoes. Deron stood inches away from the inside of his door and could hear Ms. Sylvie dragging her feet along the wooden floors. She let out a loud, mouth stretching yawn. One more thing was left and that was the closing of her door.

Deron smiled excitingly. He couldn't wait to see his Vanessa. As soon as he heard Ms. Sylvie's door closed, he quietly opened his door and edged his head out, looking for

Vanessa's light. He spotted it and tiptoed to Vanessa's door, opening it and walking in.

"Hola Papi." Vanessa whispered as the two embraced in a slow passionate kiss. Vanessa was half Puerto Rican and Deron loved her saying "Papi."

"Hey beautiful." Deron said as he held Vanessa from behind.

Both Vanessa and Deron were in their pajamas and he loved that her pajamas consisted of shorts and a t-shirt. He loved to touch her skin, rubbing it, caressing her until he could feel her eyes slowly close as if she moaned with her eyes.

"Deron sweetie?" Vanessa spoke in a calm and subdued tone.

"Yes Baby?" Deron responded as he stroked her soft and smooth skin.

"Tell me something nice."

"Anything?" Deron asked nervously.

"Yes, anything. Anything you think would fit the mood." Vanessa kept it dark in her room, other than the light she used to hint to Deron that she was ready. She also had candles lit and they were strategically placed on her old wooden dresser and on the window sill.

Raindrops were married to her windows and as they slid down the cool soothing exterior, the raindrops shed tears as they made love. The moon pierced through the window and it complimented the candle lights perfectly as the moonlight bounced perfectly off Vanessa and Deron, raindrops on the windows reflected on the faces of the two lovebirds.

"Ok baby, I'm an 18 year old virgin that's alone with the woman I love, so are you sure anything?" Deron said as Vanessa felt him smiling as he continued to hold her from behind.

"I said anything that fits the mood babe."

"Ok here goes." Deron said as he thought for a few seconds and held Vanessa tighter.

Only time can tell if my love for you can stand the test of time, but I don't need time to tell me that I am in love with you.
Only time can tell if my love for you can stand the test of time
Only your heart can beat in perfect harmony with mine
I don't need time to tell me that I'm in love with you
All I need is for our hearts to keep doing what they do
Breathe, love, kiss and beat together
And hold on tight with every change of weather
I won't accept the notion of that it's too soon for this, too soon for that love
But I will accept the constant pleading of my heart when it tells what its dreaming of
The want to beat for a lifetime beside you
The need to marinate for eternity inside you
The have to be the rhythm's of you blues
And the joy of the perfect I love you too's
Only time can tell if my love for you can stand the test of time, but I don't need time to tell me that I am in love with you.

Vanessa stood there quiet for a moment, soaking in Deron's incredible words. The moon shined directly through her window and it sparkled in her eyes. Seeing the moon bounce off Vanessa, suddenly took Deron back to the last night he had seen Janiya. He was brought back to reality when Vanessa spoke.

"Baby that was beautiful and I just love how your mind works." Vanessa whispered.

"Do you really think you are in love with me Deron?"

"Yes baby, I know I am." Deron said with confidence as he shifted Vanessa's hair from her begging neck. His lips wanted to taste her.

"If you count all the smiles that have been smiled and seen all the love that has been cherished, you will have a small sample of how I feel about you. If you've seen all the flowers in the world, or witnessed each ripple of wave in an endless ocean, then you have seen my love for you blossom effortlessly in the waves of your heart. If you have ever seen love in the eyes of a man for his lady, then you have seen but a mere fraction of the love I have for you. My love for you can be seen in my eyes, felt in my touch, heard loudly in my voice and even boisterous in my whispers and prayers, tasted upon my lips and smelled by my cologne of you."

"Deron make love to me." Vanessa whispered as tears crept down the curves of her high cheekbones. Deron turned Vanessa around so he could now face her. He kissed her like raindrops kissing the whirling winds, like the detaching of leaves from trees. He basked in the calm free flowing feeling her lips gave him.

Deron took Vanessa's hand with him as they walked to the center of her candlelit room. He began to softly whisper the song "If This World Was Mine" by Luther Vandross, one of Deron's favorite artists.

If this world were mine, I would place at your feet, all that I own. You've been so good to me, if this world were mine. I'd give you the flowers, the birds and the bees, and it'd be your love beside me, that would be all I need. If this world were mine, I'd give anything.

Deron sung while his fingers shook nervously as he unbuttoned Vanessa's pajama top. His big brown eyes got wide as if he really expected Vanessa to be wearing a bra under her top. Her head was raised to the ceiling and she silently moaned as she looked down at Deron's veins bulging in his strong hands.

Deron kneeled before her and let his lips dance to the nervous yet strong beat in his heart. They wandered aimlessly over her body and found themselves kissing her perky chocolate colored breast. Her nipples were erected to the heavens above and Deron's manhood followed. He stood and their eyes caught each other's and danced together.

As soon as Deron laid Vanessa down on her bed, a loud banging knock came from the front door.

"Deron, did you hear that?" Vanessa asked as she popped up.

"Yeah I did, what was that?"

Bang bang bang bang! The knock came again and both Vanessa and Deron scampered around looking for their clothes. The knocks came faster and harder and there was a raspy voice screaming out "HELP." Vanessa and Deron looked at each other and a missed opportunity rang in both minds. Deron snapped out of it as he sensed Ms. Sylvie coming out of her room soon.

Deron ran to the door, then ran back to Vanessa to give her a kiss. His lips hovered over Vanessa's then he ran his upper lip across her lower lip then stroking her chin. Back to the door, Deron slightly opened the door to look for Ms. Sylvie and when he didn't see her, he sprinted to his room and closed the door quietly.

Bang bang bang bang!

"Someone please help me!! Please!" The raspy scraggly voice said as coughs followed. Ms. Sylvie poked her head out of her room while holding her robe together. She walked to Deron's door and banged.

"Deron! Deron! Wake up, someone is banging at the door, come with me please." Ms. Sylvie said intensely. Deron opened his door and tried to do his best impression of a man awakening from his sleep.

Together they walked down the stairs with Deron leading the way. Ms. Sylvie hit the light switch that was hidden on the wall behind one her wall plants.

Deron hesitantly opened the door and they saw a middle aged man with long drenched dreadlocks, long black peppered beard that haven't been shaved in years. He was frail and his body shook constantly as he stood there in front of Deron and Ms. Sylvie. He wore an old torn red and blue flannel shirt and some dirty corduroy pants that didn't fit him. The man had no shoes on his feet had discolored toe nails, and blisters and cuts on them. Simply put, the old man looked like a slave that had escaped the plantation. They couldn't believe what they were seeing. This man had bruises on his face and his left eye barely stayed open.

"Please, I need your help." Deron was about to close the door in the poor man's face, but Ms. Sylvie loved to help people so she stopped him and Deron frowned at Ms. Sylvie. Deron loved to help people as well, but being a man with trust issues and being considered the man of the house, he had his own reservations about helping this man out.

"What happened to you sir?" Ms. Sylvie asked while pushing Deron away from the door.

"It's a long story, but please ma'am, may I please come in. I know it's strange for a man that looks the way I do, to come banging on your door and asking to come in, but please, I beg of you to let me in before they find me." The old man said as he brought his hands to his face, blowing in them to warm them up.

Ms. Sylvie gave him a long look up and down, still holding her robe together with one hand and holding the door with the other. Finally, she invited the man in and the old man limped his way into the home.

"Deron go get this man a warm blanket and turn the heater on. Also, make some hot cocoa please and thank you." Ms. Sylvie ordered.

"And Vanessa you and the others go back to your rooms." They followed directions, even Deron.

"Ok mister, first off what is your name and secondly,

what's going on with you?"

"Well ma'am, my name is Lawrence, Lawrence Silverman and I've been held captive against my will for over 15 years. I haven't seen my beautiful wife and daughter in the same amount of time." Lawrence said as he continued to cough. He looked over Ms. Sylvie's living room, making sure he was safe there.

"Well Mr. Silverman, I'm not sure what all happened to you, but I'm sorry it happened. The only thing I could do for you is call the police and have them come and take you so you could tell your story." Ms. Sylvie said softly.

"That is perfectly fine with me ma'am and thank you for your hospitality and letting me in, I know how hard it had to be to let a complete stranger in your home when he looks the way I do, so I sincerely thank you." Mr. Silverman said. Deron finally arrived with the blanket and hot cocoa. He offered it to Mr. Silverman and noticed something familiar about him. Deron saw a mole right in the corner of his eye brows and remembered Janiya had one in almost the exact same location and that made him think of Janiya and how much he missed her.

Deron daydreamed about Janiya until the police showed up to Ms. Sylvie's home to take Mr. Silverman away. They both watched as Mr. Silverman rode away with the policeman, wondering what would end up happening to him.

CHAPTER 13

1995 Janiya 18

Senior year was coming to an end for Janiya and she couldn't wait. No one knew anything had happened to Janiya, not even Layla. They were best friends and closer than they had ever been and Layla knew something had changed with Janiya, but she couldn't figure out what it was. She watched Janiya become angrier and more introverted than she had ever been before. Layla also wondered why Janiya had begun wearing layers of clothing and dark colors.

When she walked, she lacked confidence. Not that she really had much to begin with, but Layla just saw something different in her walk. Before, Janiya's walk was more of a slow strut with slumped shoulders and wandering eyes. Now it's more of a quick scurry while she held on tight to her possessions. Her eyes glanced nervously as she seemed to become alert and twitchy of her surroundings.

Janiya found a job at a motel and as part of her benefits, she was able to rent a room. She took all her things from her home and moved into her motel room. Luckily for her it was closer to her school.

Janiya tried in vain to continue to look and dress the same way she did before she left home, but it was becoming increasingly difficult to keep things the same without anyone knowing. She knew she just needed to make it until the last day of school. Then she could disappear off to college.

Her room was dark and had stains on the wall. The carpet had a strong odor to it. The lamp shades were the color of old dirt. The shower curtains needed to be replaced and the AC vents needed to be dusted.

There was nothing appealing about this room to Janiya and it was far from what she was used to back home. What Janiya loved most about this domicile of the poor, was it was hers. It never mattered that she continued to find something wrong with her place. Her place gave her a sense of protection and that was more important than anything else.

Janiya stood looking at herself in the bathroom mirror. Her long flowing hair was too long and had split ends in her eyes. Her gorgeous and perfectly shaped hazel eyes were too round for her liking. The barely visible bags under her eyes ate away at her already low self esteem. Her beautiful stunning smile seemed fake and forced to her and she was self conscious of her small teeth. Her beauty mole that rested just above her left eyebrow was rare to everyone else, yet Janiya wished it was rare to her as well.

Janiya picked herself apart. She was simply dazzling, but after experiencing what she experienced with Phillip, it made her question everything about herself. It made her doubt her beauty and her sex appeal. She was nasty, she was dirt and she was lower than dirt. She was unworthy of happiness and undeserving of love. She did think she had a great figure according to what she saw on TV, but she wondered who and why someone would want her body after being damaged by Phillip.

To help pass the time by, Janiya began to think about Deron and she wondered what he was doing, what he looked like, was he with anyone? She thought about making love to Deron and the tingling feeling she got gave her goose bumps.

Many times, Janiya was left wallowing in what seemed like forever in the image of Deron kissing her full soft lips. With that thought, she softly bit her lips and tasted the sweet corners of her mouth. She could even taste the sugary dew that hung from Deron's lips. Janiya could feel the thunderous beats of his heart, or maybe it was hers. She listened to the moans that formed as their lips continuously met. Janiya began to pleasure herself if her filthy room to the incredible images of Deron.

Janiya imagined tiny pants escaping her breath. With each pause, time would stand still each time Deron shifted his tongue slowly across her lower begging lip.

Janiya closed her eyes and moaned as she thought about Deron getting full from feasting upon her garden and quenching his thirst from the essence of her cascading waterfalls. She exploded on her fingers from the intense pleasure Deron brought in her mind.

She smiled at the memory of him, her heart danced at the sound of his voice in her mind and finally her heart at the thought of reuniting with Deron.

Janiya cleaned herself off and quickly grabbed a pen and paper. She jumped excitedly in the bed that she hated, but loved at the moment. She began to write Deron a letter with no intentions of him ever reading it.

Hi Deron, I can't believe I'm doing this. First off, how are you doing? Me I'm doing pretty good I guess. I miss you like crazy Deron, I miss your handsome face, your irresistible eyes and your sexy smile. I remember the feeling I had when you touched me and wow, it's giving me chills now as I write this letter. I hope you still think of me and I hope you find yourself missing me as well. Oh, I talked to Layla and she told me what happened to your parents. I'm sorry and I wish I could have been there for you because I could only imagine what was going through your mind. I have no idea where you are Deron and it's crazy, but I wish I could find you like you found me that day. That was the most romantic thing I've ever witnessed and it was the greatest night of my life. Deron, if you're out there somewhere, please come and find me again. I'm not sure how I could miss someone so much, but it makes perfect sense that it's you that I miss this much. How could something so special, so wonderful, so longed for and so treasured, be on such an undeserving mind like mine. Deron I need you right now more than ever and there are things I need to tell you that I should've told you when I had the chance. So Deron, if love is really as powerful as people say, then please find me Deron. I love you

Janiya signed and dated the letter. She stuffed it in a notebook in her backpack. She said her prayers and laid down and let the thoughts of Deron continue to fill her mind. Eventually she fell asleep.

"Hey J, you look refreshed, what got into you last night? Or should I ask who got into you?" Layla laughed.

"Someone definitely got into me girl, but not the nasty way you thinking of." Janiya chuckled as they entered the school.

"Girl ain't nothing nasty about it, shoot, it feels good. Something that feels good can't be nasty can it?" Layla asked sarcastically.

Janiya tried her best to stay in her good mood and not let the ignorant response by Layla ruin her day. Any other day, Janiya would have gone back to thinking about how nasty and dirty sex could really be when the wrong person forces themselves on you, but she digressed and kept the angelic smile on her face.

"L, I was thinking about Deron last night and he's the one that got into me."

"J, I don't get it, did he come to your house or did y'all meet up somewhere, I'm confused. You finally figured out where he was?"

"No L, not like that. Deron got inside me, inside my mind and it was great. I thought about everything we talked about, and our last encounter, which I never told you about." Janiya said while walking arm in arm with Layla.

Janiya wore a nice bright yellow sundress with white flip flops. She wore makeup for the first time all senior year and she even put a yellow flower in her hair. Her hair was wavy and flowing down her back. Janiya was numb to all of the looks she was getting from the boys because she figured they were for Layla. Today was Janiya's day and even the gorgeous Layla recognized that.

"Girl, what's gotten into you? You got makeup on, hair done and that sexy ass dress on. You don't see these boys looking at you?" Layla said as she stopped Janiya in the hallway to point all the boys out, but Janiya was high off the memory of Deron.

"L, I don't care about these boys and I doubt they care about me. If they really truly knew everything about me, trust me, they wouldn't want no parts of me. There's only one guy, one man that actually wants me, or maybe I just want him to." Janiya said leaning against her locker staring into space. Layla laughed, and snapped her fingers and begged Janiya to snap out of it.

"L, you're my best friend right?" Janiya asked.

"Of course I am J. What kind of question is that?" Layla said as she frowned.

"I know you are girl, I just need a huge favor when school ends. You know I plan on going off to school in New York as soon as this shit is over. And…and…" Janiya hesitated.

"Wait! What! You going to school where? New York? J, how can you go so far away, I got accepted to The University of Texas, so I'm staying here. We just started back hanging strong and now you're leaving." Layla screamed.

"L you don't understand, just trust me."

"Well J, get me to understand" Layla begged. Janiya continued to lean against her locker and stare out to space until she looked at Layla. She was surprised to see tears in Layla's eyes. Janiya always thought of Layla as this emotionless beauty queen so the sight of tears on her face brought tears to her own.

"L come with me, I need to tell you something." Janiya grabbed her hand and led her to the empty stairwell.

"Layla I need to tell you something that I've been dealing with for a few years now, but girl, before I do, I need you to promise me that it will stay between me and you."

"Damn girl, it must be serious because you called me Layla. Anyway girl, you know I promise, now tell me what's going on." Layla begged. Janiya eyes drooped and her shoulders slumped as she sat in the stairwell with Layla.

"Well, it all started about six years ago. I think I remember Phillip sending my mom out to the store to get something. He knocked on my door and came into my room. I…I could remember seeing the hall light on and this big man's shadow in my doorway. I had no idea what he wanted, but to make a long story short Layla, Phillip came into my room, forced himself on me and no matter how hard I tried to fight him off, nothing worked. He touched me…" Janiya began to cry uncontrollably and Layla stood against the rail holding her trembling hands over her mouth.

"He touched me and kissed me everywhere. I punched…I..I kicked, but L, it was pointless. He ripped my clothes off..and..and…" Janiya wiped her tears away and tried to finish her story. Layla hands still shook over her mouth as she couldn't believe what Janiya was telling her, but things were starting to make sense to her now. She knew something was going on with Janiya, but just couldn't put her finger on it. Janiya looked up at Layla and let out a sarcastic laugh.

"Girl, I finally decide to wear makeup and now look, I'm messing it all up. Anyway, he ripped my clothes off and forced himself inside me. He did this over and over to me throughout the years and he told me that if I ever told anyone, he would kill me. So I kept it to myself and each time he came into my room, I fought like always and like always it was pointless. So girl, the day finally came, matter of fact, do you remember the day I snapped at you for calling Phillip my dad?" Janiya asked.

"Yea girl, I remember that. I didn't know what the hell was wrong with you that day."

"Well that day I got fed up, so I decided to tell somebody. I decided to tell the one person you think would always protect you. Who would always keep you out of harm. The one person you knew would always be there." Janiya stared out into space as the students walked passed her in the stairwell.

"I finally had built up enough courage to tell my mom." Janiya said as she smacked her teeth in the direction of Layla and shook her head.

"Well what did she say Janiya?" Layla asked. The makeup on both girls faces were ruined by the tears. Layla finally pulled out some Kleenex from her pink Coach bag and offered some to the bawling Janiya.

"What did she say?" Layla sniffed.

"What did she say? She couldn't say anything, but Phillip said what she couldn't say."

"Wait, he was there while you told your mother J?" Layla screamed while finally kneeling down next to Janiya.

"Shhh, girl don't be so loud, but yea he was there."

"Ok so what did he say?" Layla whispered. Janiya sat there for a few moments shaking her head as if she was reliving the moment. The warning bell rang for the students to get to their class and Layla's head popped up, knowing they didn't have much longer to talk.

"L, talk to me girl, what did Phillip say?"

"He said…he said…" Janiya found it hard to let it out. She buried her head in her lap and Layla held her while she cried uncontrollably.

"He said that she knew the whole time Layla. He said that my mother, not my friend, not a stranger, not the grocery lady, not that lady over there, or over there, but he said my mother, the lady that gave birth to me, the lady that carried me for 9 months, the lady that supposedly loved me, the lady I thought would never hurt me. He said this lady knew the whole time." Janiya cried out while becoming more and more animated and Layla tried her best to get her to calm down, all the while in shock herself.

"J, I don't know what to tell you. I had no clue of what you were dealing with at home and girl, this just proves that we think we pay attention to people, but we never really truly know what they may have going on in their lives. Girl I'm so sorry, I just can't believe this. Why didn't you ever tell me? I could have told my dad. You know he works in the force too, I'm sure he could have done something." Layla said.

"L, what would you have done? What would you have done if it were you? Trust me, when something like that happens, you don't know who to trust, you don't know what to say and eventually a point came when I thought it was my fault. Hell, some parts of me still believe it was my fault. Anyway girl, look, this final bell is about to ring so let me get back to that favor I need from you." Janiya said, wiping the tears away from her now ruined face. Her eyes were swollen, dried up tears rested on her face and she knew she was going to be late to her class because there was no way she was going to class looking the way she does.

"Ok J, what is it?"

"I wrote this letter to Deron yesterday and at first, I wrote it just to be writing. I didn't want him to read it, but with me leaving for New York as soon as school is out, I'm sure you would see him well before I would. So I need you to hold on to this and promise me you will give it to him next time you see him."

"Ok J, you know I still think you can do a lot better than Deron and I have no idea what you see in him, but I promise you, I will give him your letter if I see him." Layla said as she took the letter.

"L, didn't you just say that you never really know what a person may be going through? You have no real reasons to hate Deron, or dislike him other than the fact that the other kids did, but I don't have time to get into this with you so please just do me that one favor." Janiya said and walked off, leaving Layla standing on the steps of the cold stairwell.

CHAPTER 14

1997

It was the best she had in a long time. Mr. Rob Tittle always put it down on Janiya, but this time, he left her there panting with her mouth dripping out moans. She was still left in the same doggy style position he left her after he exploded inside her.

The 26 year old Rob Tittle had the body of a Greek God. He was from Brooklyn, New York and had the thickest Brooklyn accent. He stood 6'4 and weighed 230 pounds of solid muscle. His green eyes caught Janiya's attention. She wanted him ever since falling deep in his hypnotizing eyes. He had lengthy deep, pitch black, curly hair and wore it in cornrows. Rob had a light, caramel complexion and he had muscles on top of muscles.

High cheekbones and a chiseled jaw line drove Janiya crazy, by far the most physically blessed man that Janiya has been with. Those good looks came with a curse. Janiya's eyes couldn't help but maneuver up and down Rob's beautifully molded body. She got weak every time she saw the veins bulging out of his arms. Her tongue marched its way around her lips when she saw the sweat dripping down his chest.

Janiya laid there as if she was cemented in that position while Rob followed his routine. After sex, he always went to the bathroom to wipe himself off, or do only God knows what, and it always bothered her. In the 2 years that they have been together, she had never brought it up to Rob.

Janiya was an attractive, strong, and intelligent, black woman. With the past she's had, being raped and molested by her stepfather, insecurities wore on her like a new layer of unwanted skin.

Growing up, Janiya never felt wanted by her mom, but she never knew why and from what she remembered, it started soon after her biological father was killed. Janiya would tell you, as she told several people. Her life has been hell ever since the day Phillip knocked on her mother's door to give the bad news about her father.

It was possible that she lost the one guy that she loved, Deron. She was molested and raped by her step father and to add to the turmoil in her life, she found out that her mom knew about it the entire time. Not once stepping in as her mother and protector, to stop Phillip. That more than anything, had the biggest effect on Janiya.

She's has had numerous boyfriends and has been living an unstable life, full of alcohol and sex. She was even dabbling in the world of drugs.

Janiya finally was able to lay down in her California king size bed, after being immovable from her doggy style position that Rob left her in. She cuddled up with her blanket with no hint of clothes caressing her body. She wondered why Rob was still in the bathroom. She wanted him with her, but she knew he wouldn't give her what she wanted. Janiya wanted to be held.

That was something she always wanted, but had never

gotten from Rob. Janiya couldn't stand it any longer and her eyes grew tight, and she bit her fingernails in anticipation of confronting Rob who was obviously full of activity in the bathroom.

Tiptoeing her way to the bathroom door, Janiya pinned her ears to the door to see if she could get a clue of what was going on with Rob on the other side of door. Her eyes were looking down toward the hardwood floors as she concentrated hard to hear something, anything.

The slow sensual moans that Janiya heard angered her to the point where her eyes grew angled, her jaws clenched and her hands slowly grasped the door knob, then letting go when she figured it was locked.

Rob had to have forgotten that Janiya was the most persistent person that anyone could ever know and she could easily work her way to picking a simple door lock.

Janiya tiptoed back to the door after she got a credit card out of her purse. She slid the card through the door and with little effort, the door popped open. Janiya's eyes couldn't get any bigger and her mouth couldn't have opened wider.

She watched Rob finish the job that she obviously couldn't accomplish. Rob stood hanging over the sink naked with his penis clenched strongly in his right hand. Janiya couldn't believe he was masturbating minutes after having sex with her. He tried desperately to grab his pants while Janiya watched him as tears fell.

"So I guess you had to come in here and finish since I couldn't do it for you?" Janiya said. Her big eyes and wide mouth had returned back to form.

"Damn it ain't even like that. Why a nigga can't get no privacy?" Rob screamed back in defense.

Many emotions were ran through Janiya's mind and she was clearly pissed, but turned on at the same time. Quickly she snapped out of it when he walked by trying to button his pants.

"What's the problem Rob? If I don't do it for you, what are you here for because I can be with someone who believes I'm just enough for him." Janiya screamed as she followed Rob while he tried to escape to another room.

He disregarded her questions and strolled into the kitchen grabbing a drink of water.

"Janiya you know damn well you ain't going nowhere. Every day I gotta hear about you talking that shit about going to somebody else." Rob said while he twisted the cap off his bottled water.

"What did you say to me?" Janiya said not really surprised about what Rob said because she's heard it before.

"I mean you cute and all, but who's really gon want you?" You're overweight and shit yo' sex game is just aight. You know I'm the best thing that's happened to you. You know damn well I ain't going nowhere and you not going to somebody else. All this shit you talking about is unnecessary." Rob said. He leaned against the granite countertop as he took sips of water.

There was zero emotion in his voice, no care in his expression, no thought to his words before he spoke. Janiya refused to go back and forth with Rob because the humiliated side of Janiya knew Rob was right. She didn't agree with his statement that she wouldn't go another man. She did agree with Rob about her weight because every since she left home, she hadn't been taking care of herself. Janiya's once stunning, model like frame had now become a shame to her.

Rob had abused Janiya's self esteem so much that she truly believed everything he told her. She believed no one else wanted her and she believed that Rob was the best she could do. A pitiful, sorry man is better than no man at all, right? Love has been a long time coming for Janiya and she remembered the times when she begged God for a thing called love. It's been so long that she had tricked herself into believing that Rob loved her.

"Everyone loves differently." That was her justification.

If you have to trick yourself into believing something is love, then most likely, it's not love. One day Janiya would see it. For now, she would reside in the artificial home of false love.

Tears ran down Janiya's emotionally damaged face while she watched Rob stare at her in disgust. Rob's eyes grew immense and he threw his hands out in front of him.

"What? Why are you just staring at me Janiya? Don't you have to get ready for work?"

"Yea, I guess so, since I'm the only one that pays the bills up in here." Janiya mumbled as she walked away. Rob heard her, but didn't care. He finished off his bottle of water and followed Janiya into the bedroom.

"Baby, come here." Rob said as he reached out for Janiya's arm. Janiya wiped her eyes before turning around, but her eyes were still filled with tears.

"Baby, I'm sorry, you know I am. I just have a lot of things going on and I'm stressed out. I'm trying to find a job, you know it's been hard on me since I got out baby, but a nigga trying ya' know?" Rob said. He caressed Janiya's smooth hands.

She couldn't stop the tears from cascading down the curves of her cheeks. She had been hearing that story for 2 years now and Janiya still believed there's some truth to it.

Rob always reeled Janiya back in by comforting her. To her, that proved Rob indeed loved her. It was different love, but to Janiya, it was still love.

"I know baby, but I just can't believe you was doing that in the bathroom. Do you do that every time after sex?" Janiya asked while Rob wiped her tears away.

"Well baby, to be honest, it's not the first time I've done it. It's just the first time you caught me." Rob said.

More tears escaped Janiya's eyes and she tried to get away, but Rob's strength kept her there.

"Let me go Rob." Janiya cried.

"Baby, what's wrong? I'm just being honest with you. You always telling a nigga to be honest and when I do, you can't take it." Rob screamed as he threw Janiya's hand away in anger.

Tears continued to run away from Janiya's eyes while she watched Rob go on his rant.

"Rob you can't choose what you want to be honest about. Since you're so honest, tell me are you cheating on me? Do you love me? Are you using me?" Janiya screamed back while she stood face to face to Rob.

"Those are the questions I want honest answers to Rob."

Janiya continued while Rob stood against the dresser with his arms folded. Janiya was pissed. She was so pissed that she didn't notice how Rob's biceps bulged. She had an evil red look in her eyes and she wanted answers. Not any answers but honest ones.

Rob wrestled back and forth in his mind whether to tell her the truth or not. He knew whether he did or not, Janiya wasn't going anywhere. He knew that he had Janiya exactly where he wanted her.

Rob was irresistible in Janiya's eyes and sadly for Janiya, Rob knew it and he used it to his advantage. Scratching his scalp, just in between the parts of his corn rolls, Rob was trying his best to stay calm, but Janiya's voice continued to get louder and louder. Janiya kept crying, but it was no longer sad tears that were leaking out, they were angry tears.

"Fine." Rob screamed.

"Fine what?" Janiya replied. She backed off as she wiped her tears away.

"Ask me any question you want Janiya and I promise you I will give you an honest answer." Rob said still as he stood against the old mahogany dresser.

"You already know the questions Rob, so don't ask me to ask you again." Janiya screamed, side-eyed at Rob. Her hands rested on her thick hips. The 19 inch television was on, but was low enough that it didn't interrupt the argument. The squeaky ceiling fan refused to produce enough air to keep Janiya from sweating.

"Fine Janiya, yes I'm cheating on you and yes I'm using you because you allow me to. I care about you Janiya, but no I don't love you." Janiya sat motionless on the bed with a blank expression on her face.

There wasn't any added anger because they were answers she already knew deep down.

"Now what Janiya? What did this information do for you? Once again, you know I'm not going anywhere so why did you want this information. Be careful what you fucking ask for Janiya because you just may get it. Now hurry up and get ready so you won't be late for work. Brang a nigga something back to eat later on since you didn't make me no breakfast this morning." Janiya sat there on her bed still motionless and despondent as she watched Rob slip on a t-shirt and leave her house.

How many times can she tell herself "I pay the bills around here." She was livid with Rob, but more at herself because she created this monster and has no wanting way of wanting to destroy it because she's living and dying by her motto 'Stupid, pitiful man is better than no man at all'.

CHAPTER 15

1997

"I don't know who chose me to speak at this thing, but I'll say thank you for the opportunity. I'm not exactly sure what to say."

Deron said as he nervously stood on the podium for Ms. Sylvie's funeral. The now 20 year old Deron stood a ripped 6 foot 6 inches 245 pounds. His pearly white teeth complimented his clean cut goatee. The smooth, caramel skin of Deron glistened when he smiled. One deep dimple showed up on his face just by simply talking. All of the ladies loved for Deron to talk just to watch his dimple. He had perfectly shaped eyebrows with long eyelashes. One leg seemed to drag slowly when he walked, but it was the sexiest part of Deron.

Deron was known for always being calm and knowing the right thing to say at the right time, but here at Ms. Sylvie's funeral, he was at a loss for words. Sweating profusely and stuttering was out of character for Deron.

Ms. Sylvie was Deron's mother the last few years and he loved her more than anything. He loved her more than his own mother, more than Janiya and more than his girlfriend Vanessa.

"I never really handled..ummm..death too well. Well let me rephrase that. I probably handled it too well, according to some people. I always believed that to truly allow someone to rest in peace, you should only remember the good times and not worry about them no longer being here. What I didn't realize until now, is that I've never lost anyone that's meant so much to me until now and now I'm trying my best not collapse up here. Not too many people know my story and I promise I'll be brief when I tell it. My childhood started off pretty normal. I had a mom and dad under one roof and we were the family that people in the hood were jealous of, but life got in the way ya' know. My dad lost his job and couldn't find another one. My mom got introduced to drugs while my dad found a new friend at the bottom of his alcohol bottle. He would get drunk and beat my mom senseless and she would get so high that I doubt she even felt the beatings. One night in particular, I snuck out of my home and when I came back home, my father had a gun pointing directly at my mother. Long story short, my dad killed my mom and then was shot dead by a police officer. I had no clue of what caused it to the point where my dad pulled out a gun. I was taken away and was placed with Ms. Sylvie, and this woman…."

Deron paused. He removed his glasses from face to wipe the steady flow of tears.

Vanessa watched Deron struggle with his speech, but all of sudden she stared out into space and no longer hung onto

Deron's words. Vanessa wore a black knee length pen striped skirt with a black silk blouse, black pumps and thin glasses that matched Deron's. Her hair laid softly down her back and her makeup was flawless. She excused herself and Deron tried not to focus on the reason she was leaving.

"Without this woman, I'm not sure where I'd be and I truly mean that. She allowed me to express myself, she allowed me to finally be myself. Not only did she allow it, she almost required me to be no one other than who was. I will forever be indebted to her. She always begged for me to call her mother or mom, but for some reason I continued to call her Ms. Sylvie and I'm not sure why. Well mom, if you're listening, I love you and I miss you. You showed me what life and living was all about and I will always love you for that." Deron continued to cry as he ended his speech and he finally exited the podium. Deron went to the white casket with roses sitting on top and looked inside.

Ms. Sylvie died of leukemia and in a way, Deron was happy to see it all over with. She was no longer in pain and she no longer had to suffer. As he saw her lying there in her favorite pink dress, Deron smiled and walked away.

Finally, the funeral was over and people were scampering all over. Some found their way over to Deron to thank him for his speech. Throughout all of the hugs and handshakes, Deron looked for Vanessa, but couldn't find her anywhere.

"Deron is that you?" A gorgeous woman asked.

"Wow time has definitely been great to you." The woman said.

"I'm sorry, I don't know you, but thank you." Deron said. He narrowed his eyes trying desperately to remember who this beautiful person was, but nothing registered. The eye-catching woman placed her hands on her hips and smiled, shocked that Deron couldn't remember who she was.

"Deron, it's me Layla." Layla screamed.

"Layla from....?"

"Wow, you really don't remember me do you?" Layla said, starting to get offended.

"Well, I know you remember Janiya. I'm her best friend and we use to always be together in school." Layla said. Up until she said Janiya's name, Deron had no clue of who the attractive woman was, but she was gorgeous to him.

Layla was stunning as usual, and Deron was the kind of guy that recognized beauty, but when he finally realized who she was, the attraction went away.

"Oh, Layla, ok I remember. Sorry about that, but I'm sure you can remember that I was quite the outsider back then." Deron said and they both laughed.

"Yes Lord, I remember that, but what I don't remember is you being this handsome." Layla said and Deron wondered if that was supposed to be a compliment.

"Well, how are you doing? Still good-looking I see." Deron said while stuffing his hand in his pocket and leaning up against the beige colored wall.

"I'm doing good, but let's stop the small talk, I know you want to ask about Janiya so go right ahead."

"Well, how is she?" Deron was beginning to get pretty short with Layla since he remembered what all she did and what all she said about him when they were kids. He was the type to hold grudges and not forgive so easily, so he was growing increasingly frustrated when talking with Layla.

"She's doing ok, I guess, I hadn't really talked to her much over the last two years. I do know she's in New York going to school."

Deron's eyes wandered away and he began to think about her, not that he ever stopped. Here lately, he began to think of Janiya more and more. He wondered if she was ok and where she was.

Vanessa was his girlfriend, but passion in their relationship was lacking. There was a saying that Deron always believed in, 'Do everything with passion, if the passion is not there, go where the passion is present.'

"So Layla, how did you know Ms. Sylvie?" Deron asked.

"I didn't really know her, but my dad knew her very well. She was always the person he recommended kids go to when needing a foster home. So, I'm here to support my father." Layla said as she pointed to her dad.

"Oh ok, well Layla look. Let's not pretend here ok? You didn't like me back then and I knew everything you said about me. So right now I'm trying my best not to say to you what I really want to say. Let's just walk away ok? I don't want this day to get any worse than it already is." Deron said as he stood straight up with his hands still wedged in his pockets.

Not really giving Layla a chance to reply, Deron attempted to walk away, but surprisingly Layla stopped him.

"Deron, you're right ok. I never really liked you. I said some things about you before I even knew anything about you and I apologize for that. That's not the reason I came up to talk to you. It's not about you and it's not about me. It's about Janiya. Look, she told me some things about what she was dealing with and I really feel like she needs you. Even though that was a couple years ago, something tells me she could really use you right now." Layla said as sincerely as possible. Deron eyes angled at Layla once again as he sipped his cool drink that was brought to him.

"What are you talking about? What's wrong with Janiya?" Deron screamed, forgetting where he was. He quickly lowered his voice, sat his drink down, and stepped closer to Layla. He placed his strong hands on Layla's slender arm.

"Deron, I don't feel right being the one to tell you. I know you don't like me, but please find her, that's what she would want. Deron please just find Janiya! Look, dad is waving me over. Deron, I have to go." Layla left Deron there with his mouth opened wide. She left him there the same way a good writer left their readers wanting more.

Deron wanted more information and before he could say anything, Layla stopped suddenly.

"Oh! Deron, I almost forgot. Janiya gave me a letter she wrote you about two years ago and I promised her that if I ever saw you, I would give it to you. I made sure that whenever I left the house, I had this letter with me because she would kill me if she knew I saw you and I didn't give it to you. So here you go Deron and please remember what I told you." Layla said as she hugged Deron without him reciprocating it. Deron just stared at the letter that Layla placed in his now sweaty hands.

Layla walked away for good and just as Deron looked up, Vanessa came walking towards him. He stuffed the letter in his back pocket and rushed towards Vanessa when he saw that she had been crying.

"Vanessa baby, what's wrong? Have you been crying?" Deron asked while hugging the distraught Vanessa.

"Deron, we need to talk now, is there anywhere we can go?" Vanessa cried. Deron sighed deeply. He shook his head and his shoulders slumped while he thought to himself, 'Could the day get any worse?'

CHAPTER 16

2001

Over the past four years, Deron had been searching endlessly to find reasons to go to New York to look for his true love. Not a day went by where he didn't daydream about Janiya. Not a second went by that he didn't yearn for the touch of the person he knew had his heart.

Deron was out enjoying the beautiful Texas weather at his favorite park. The sunlight beamed off his smooth skin and with Deron wearing a sleeveless, fitted shirt, the nearby women bit their lips as they watched his arms bulge. He was fresh from a workout and instead of sweat, the ladies saw Deron glistening in the sun. They tried desperately to keep from partaking in taking a bite out of the sexy Deron. Unfortunately for the ladies, he only had one person on his mind and his manhood became hard. It became inflexible and reached for the sky when Janiya danced around in his memories.

She constantly danced elegantly, passionately in the fruits of Deron's heart. She wandered willfully, joyfully inside his self proclaimed lost mind that Vanessa brought him to. Somehow Janiya, without being visible, made it seem normal while she was resided in his mind.

There was no way Deron wanted Janiya to leave a place that was all his, but a place he often wanted to escape. As long as she was there, his mind was at peace. He mentally pulled her close, imagining her head becoming one with his chest. His heartbeat created the beautiful melodies that left Janiya's eyes sealed together and left him to wander in her mind as she wandered in his. They saw each other in each other's heart and read each other's thoughts.

Deron's heart rejoiced and showered excited tears while his mind made the soothing sounds of water clapping against the riverbanks. It applauded his choice of lifelong love to reside there. What a dancer Janiya was.

The day of Ms. Sylvie's funeral about four years ago, Vanessa dropped a bomb on Deron after hearing his speech and his heart hadn't recovered. He already had trust issues, already had been betrayed many times before and he had no clue how to let go of the moment. It replayed back over in his mind

"Deron, baby we need to talk." Deron remembered Vanessa saying while holding his hands, yet never making eye contact with him.

"Spit it out Vanessa, I'm already having a tough day, so whatever it is, no matter how bad, just spit it out."

"Ok, Deron. After listening your speech about what happened to you when you were younger...I..I..." Vanessa stuttered, her lips trembled nervously and tears began to fall uncontrollably.

"When I was younger? You mean when I talked about my dad killing my mom?" Deron asked. Vanessa shook her head yes with her eyes closed.

"I know what happened that night Deron." Vanessa said as her cries became louder.

Deron remembered people in the church began staring and wondering what was going on. He tried his best to calm her down, but nothing helped.

"Baby, what do you mean you know what happened?" Deron whispered in the troubled ears of Vanessa.

"Deron, I know what happened."

"Ok, I don't understand why you're crying. I mean, I can understand if you knew of the situation, but you're just now realizing that it was my parents, right?" Deron shook his head hoping Vanessa would say yes.

"Baby I can't be mad if you're just now realizing it was my parents, so come on babe, stop crying." Deron whispered as he wiped her tears away, but Vanessa still couldn't look at Deron. She mumbled something under her breath while shaking her head and hugging Deron.

"Baby, what did you say? I can't hear you."

"Deron, I said I knew. I been knowing. I been knowing it was your parents. Baby, I saw how it all happened." Deron's jaws clenched and he drew back from Vanessa.

"What do you mean you knew and you've always known? How long have you known about this Vanessa?" Deron whispered.

"I've known since you first came to Ms. Sylvie's foster home Deron. She and I knew, but don't be mad at Ms. Sylvie. She kept trying to get me to tell you Deron, but I never knew how." Vanessa said softly.

"So, 'Deron I know how everything happened that night' was hard to say?" Deron questioned while looking around pretending to be civil.

"So, exactly what happened that night?" Deron asked. Vanessa repeatedly shook her head until she finally blurted it out. She sighed as if she a huge boulder was lifted off of her shoulders.

"Deron your mother caught your dad sleeping with my mom, my prostitute mom. My mom was in your home Deron, and your mom caught them in the act." Deron's fists were balled and he walked away, leaving the church. He didn't know what he was more upset at, hearing what started the argument that night, or knowing that Vanessa kept something from him. She knew how he felt about honesty and betrayal.

Even with reliving that moment, Deron frowned momentarily, but was brought out of it because of Janiya. He allowed love to be his blind music. He allowed the melodies in his head to erase that thought from his memory so that he could focus on Janiya.

Deron let his love for Janiya soothe his mind so that he could feel all the good vibes from all of the instruments of love. Deron closed his eyes and imagined Janiya laying her head against his chest. He wanted her to feel his heartbeat and pretend it was the rhythm and blues of love's soul ballads. He allowed the senses to take him on a journey on love's train.

Deron became numb to the outside forces. He became blind to life's hard courses and he just heard the music of love. He kept his eyes closed so he could feel Janiya, feel the color of love, the sound of love and how it grooved inside Janiya while allowing her to see even when she's blind. Deron sat there on the bench watching the waves in the small lake, and allowed his mind to dance away to love.

CHAPTER 17

Leaves ran away from each other in the wind as Deron wrapped up another writing session at his favorite park. The water rippled from strong gusts and clouds formed angels and animals in the sky. Deron wore his favorite burnt orange University of Texas sweatpants, fitted white tee shirt, and ball cap. His aged running shoes matched his sweatpants perfectly. He wore sunglasses even though the only sign of sunshine was in his heart because of his thoughts of Janiya.

Before closing his red, wrinkled notebook, Deron stood and looked far out into the lake. He watched the sailboats slowly sail in the distance and saw flocks of ducks. He imagined himself being one of the ducks and having a family, but Deron was brought back to the harsh realm of his solitude.

Other than Vanessa, Deron was alone. He didn't have brothers, sisters, aunts or uncles. Even Vanessa was slipping through his grasp, even though it was he that was unclenching the grasp.

Deron began to see Janiya in front of him allowed his five senses to become the eye glasses to his mind, only focused on her. What a sight for Deron's eyes. Open or closed, he could see images of himself exploring her world. He would plant seeds in her oceans while she rained on his nature.

Deron laughed to himself as he wondered who said you couldn't hear the sounds of the most gentle of touch. He could hear the moans escape Janiya's breath. He could hear her as she heard the sounds of him breathing, better yet, panting while hovering inches from her goosebumps.

Deron imagined allowing a single touch to engulf her body with the power only he could possess. He would touch her universe and her heart would orgasm, spilling all over him.

Feeling her touch, Deron's taste buds were going crazy, begging, saying 'Deron you know what we want'. He stood there with his eyes closed while his mind wandered. Mentally, he let his taste buds suffer while he imagined tasting the pulse of Janiya's neck, the curve of her lips, the rise of her breast, the peaks of her nipples and the throbbing of her inner thighs. Finally, Deron gave into his taste buds. He allowed the tip and then the spread of his tongue to play. Deron paused and licked his lips. The thought of tasting Janiya was too good to finish his thought, but he managed.

His manhood erected, throbbed, and pulsated while daydreaming about experiencing the sweetness of Janiya's exuberant, moistened garden as he deep sea dove inside her ocean. He would rise up, drenched in her love, heart racing, and tongue dragging while panting, but still wanting more

He could smell her essence and her presence, even being so far away from her. Deron felt her right in front of him. He's seen her, heard her, smelled her and touched her so many a times that her scent clung to him like new cologne.

Deron smelled the scent of her love when he imagined

her looking at him, when she spoke to him, when she heard him and when she tasted him.

His eyes popped opened as he mentally climaxed. Deron folded his notebook together and walked away after getting himself so worked up. He adjusted his discombobulated ball cap and started on his trail home. On his journey, he saw an old rustic shed. There was an old tractor in the yard with rusty gasoline tanks around it. The shed had one small window and missing shingles on the roof. It was a big lot of land, but Deron still heard unpleasant sounds.

Deron cautiously approached the fence with the 'No Trespassing' sign dangling from it. As Deron got closer and closer it was clear to him what the sounds were. He heard begging moans from a man and Deron looked around to see who was nearby. To his liking, there was no one around paying him any attention. Deron scanned the area one more time then hopped over the corroded fence. Deron ran quickly up to the shed and was able to make out the cries as he got closer.

He pushed his ear against the cool shed and he was certain something was going on inside and he was determined help whoever it was that was in trouble.

CHAPTER 18

After hours of searching of ways to get inside the shed, Deron finally made it in. It was dark, but there was little daylight left. The only light Deron had was seeping through the small crack in the window.

There were old, torn bus seats covered in dust and spider webs. There was also an, old turned over antique kitchen stove. Rust covered the stove, which was also infested with spider webs. What Deron saw, was something out of a movie. There wasn't a place on the ground where Deron was able to walk freely. He stepped and hopped over coke cans, old car parts and plumbing pipes.

He made his way through the rubble and heard the moans again and followed the sounds. Deron walked slowly while keeping his eyes wide open incase anything were to jump out.

After walking by an old broken down bbq gril, old rakes and shovels, Deron turned around to see shelves full of old children's toys. What he saw next made him cover his mouth and step back.

Deron saw an elderly man tied to an old wooden post.

The scent of urine stung his nose. The sight of this man broke Deron's heart and nothing else entered his mind except setting this man free. One thing was evident, whoever this man was. He had been there for some years and had been starved to near death. The man was sweating profusely and his clothes were drenched in dirt with dried sweat and old blood stains. This man was in worse condition than a homeless man and whoever was holding him captive was doing the perfect job of just doing the bare minimum to keep him alive.

His dreadlocks had an odor and beard was shiny peppered and matted. He was a dark skinned man and wrinkles fitted tightly to his skin, giving no signs of going anywhere. Blisters rested on his dry lips while the rope tied around his mouth gave no hint of loosening.

His eyes struggled to stay open and bounced when he tried to look up to Deron. He finally kneeled before the old man to help him out. Just as he did, he felt his cell phone buzzing in his pocket. He was sure it was Vanessa calling to check in since hours had passed the usual time Deron came home from his writing session.

Deron first found a corroded knife to cut the rope from around the old man's mouth. Just as he did, he saw just how badly cracked the man's skin was around his mouth. Deron stood to look around and he found a sink. Deron quickly, yet quietly stepped over the cob webbed wreckage in the shed to get the old man something to drink.

He held a dingy cup up to the man's mouth and lifted his chin so he drink. The old man looked up at Deron and realized he had seen him once before.

"Thank you." The old man coughed.

"Who did this to you sir?" Deron whispered as he saw chains attached to the man's hands and feet.

"The keys are in that small treasure like box on the shelf above the sink." The man coughed again. His voice was raspy and dry.

Deron got the keys and unlocked the locks attached to the chains. He quietly untangled them to set the man free, but the old man still sat there, not knowing he was liberated.

"Who did this to you?" Deron asked again.

"Man." The old man replied. Deron gave him more water and the more he drank, the crisper his voice became.

"If we're gonna leave, we need to do it now." The old man replied while looking in his cup for more water.

"Ok, let's go so I can take you to the police. Then you can tell them what happened." Deron said, looking away to make sure they were still alone.

"We can't do that. We can't do that." The man said as he placed his arms across his mouth while he coughed.

"Why? We need to." Deron whispered.

"We just can't, now if you're gonna get me outta here, we need to go now."

"Where will I take you? I have to take you to the police."

"Deron, we can't go to the cops because they were the ones that did this to me." The man said. Deron stood quickly, knocking over old, used paint cans. He pierced his eyes at the old man and his hands suddenly made a fist as he wondered how the old man knew his name.

"What the fuck. How do you know name?" Deron said as his jaws compressed.

"Can we leave first? Please. They will be coming soon." The man said with his head down, no longer having the energy to hold his head high at Deron.

"Fuck no! You tell me right now how in the hell you know my name! If you wanna get outta here, you tell me how the hell you know my name man." Deron voice began to get louder and louder. The old man sat there raising his eyes to Deron while his chin still rested on his chest.

"Deron, I came to your home one rainy night. You opened the door and Ms. Sylvie let me in. I had escaped from this place and ran to the first home I saw that was good enough distance away from this place. I got back here because you guys called the cops and the cops that picked me up were the same ones that are responsible for putting me here. So Deron, if we're gonna get outta here, we have to go now and you can't take me to the police."

Deron's eyes widened, not believing what he just heard. He began looking the man over then finally remembering the mole in the corner of his eyebrows, the dreadlocks, and the raspy voice. Deron remembered the night at Ms. Sylvie's house.

Deron took off his shoes and placed them on the old man's bruised and badly damaged feet. He stood the man up and they escaped to Deron and Vanessa's home.

CHAPTER 19

It was a cold thanksgiving weekend in Fort Worth, Texas at Deron and Vanessa's two bedroom apartment. Deron and the old man had become pretty close since Deron opened his home up to him. He cleaned the old man up and got rid of the old knotted dread locks that had a horrible stench to them. Deron took him to local thrift stores and bought him clothes, shoes and even got him a job down at the library where Deron worked.

He was a 51 year old man that spent 24 years away from his wife and daughter. Lawrence Silverman had finally opened up to Deron about what happened to him. It had been 6 months since Deron helped Lawrence escape the place he thought he would ultimately die in.

Deron set Lawrence up to attend counseling sessions since he had issues that needed to be dealt with in order to become something close to normal again. He would go to a good friend of Vanessa's twice a week at no charge. She told the psychologist everything that happened with Lawrence and how he couldn't go to the cops. She agreed to help Lawrence out and keep everything confidential.

Deron also tried, and to get Lawrence to tell him what

happened, but he didn't want to keep pushing him. The two men were having drinks on Deron's dark brown microfiber couch, and finally Lawrence was starting to open up.

Deron just sat back drinking his Bud light quietly. He allowed Lawrence to get everything off of his chest. He could tell it was hard for Lawrence, so he just waited however long it took him to start talking.

Lawrence leaned back in the most comfortable seat in the house. A seat normally reserved for Deron. He folded his hands behind his head and stared out into space.

It was a routine stop in 1979 on a dark and rainy back road in Dallas, Texas when Lawrence Silverman, a 27 year old truck driver and family man, was pulled over. Lawrence was a short and slender built man, standing 5 foot 9 inches and weighing a good 145 pounds. He had coffee brown skin and had hair everywhere on his body.

Right above his bushy right eyebrow was a hidden mole and his high cheekbones and chiseled jaw line went perfectly with his full beard. He had a slight limp to his walk because he was born with his left leg slightly longer than his right. No one knew that because he made the walk as sexy as possible.

Lawrence looked in his side mirrors of his big 18 wheeler and saw that he indeed was being pulled over, but had no idea why.

Two officers got out their dark blue cop car, leaving the lights flashing in the pitch black night.

"Hi sir, could you please get out of the vehicle?" The officer demanded.

"Hello officer. Sure, but could you tell me what I did please?" Lawrence asked with a confused look on his face. He knew his tags were current and all the lights on his rig were replaced earlier that day, so it couldn't be that. He knew he wasn't speeding and hadn't been drinking, so he had no clue why he was being pulled over.

"Sir, just do as I asked and step out the vehicle please." The officer demanded more forcefully.

Lawrence sighed loudly to let his frustration be known and he shook his head as he attempted turn his vehicle off.

"Please just get out of the vehicle sir. I did not ask you to turn it off. Follow directions sir and just get out of the truck." The officer screamed while clutching his pistol.

The other officer was a trainer and was being shown the ropes by his best friend and Captain in the Dallas Police Department, Captain Phillip Brakens.

"I'm Captain Brakens and that is Officer Davis over there, he is currently in training." Captain Brakens explained before being cut off by Lawrence.

"I understand that, but why is that important to me Captain? Can you please tell me why I'm being pulled over and why I was asked to get out of my vehicle?" Lawrence asked as his jaws tightened and his already angled eyes became even more drawn in.

"Well sir, I have reason to believe that you have been drinking?" Captain Brakens said.

"Drinking? Me? Drinking? You can't be serious. I just pulled on to the road from the gas station and I haven't had anything to drink but soda officer. So what is this really about?" Lawrence asked.

"Sir, please change your tone and walk over here so Officer Davis can give you some simple test to gauge your sobriety."

"No! I have no reason to do those tests and I already told you sir, I just pulled on this road and had nothing but fucking soda to drink. So until you give me a real reason as to why you pulled me over on this dark road, I will not be walking over to you, nor performing any sobriety test. I know my rights."

"Do as you're told or you will be going to jail tonight." The trainee Officer Davis screamed in the face of Lawrence. Lawrence turned his back on him and he was hit upside the head with his club.

"What are you doing?" Captain Brakens screamed at the trainee as they both watched Lawrence lay motionless on the ground.

"He wasn't listening, so I punished him. Don't get your panties in a wad, you're the Captain, I'm sure you can fix this some way." Officer Davis said while Captain Brakens tried to get Lawrence to respond, but was unsuccessful.

"Shit! All I tried to do was get you a little experience on a boring night and now look at what you did. There's no way I can fix this because it's on video from the car asshole." Captain Brakens whispered so his voice wouldn't get picked up also.

"Is he dead?" Officer Davis asked.

"No he's not dead, but when he wakes up from being unconscious, he's gonna remember everything and then we both will be in deep shit." Captain Brakens said kneeling beside Lawrence and looking up at Officer Davis.

"Well..." Officer Davis said while kneeling down next to Captain Brakens.

"Well what?"

"Well don't let him wake up then."

"What are you suggesting we do here?" Captain Brakens asked with frustration in his voice. This was supposed to be training for Officer Davis. It was only supposed to be a routine stop, then sending Lawrence on his way. He tried to give his trainee some experience, but it turned into something much worse. Captain Brakens was forced to do something he never thought he would.

Bang! Officer Davis hit Lawrence in the head again with his club.

"What the fuck are you doing man?" Captain Brakens screamed.

"Phillip, you know what we have to do and it has to stay between the two of us." Officer Davis said as both officers stood over Lawrence. Blood spilled from Lawrence's head. He laid unconscious and was possibly dead. Captain Brakens knew something had to be done.

Lawrence had reminisced for a good two hours and Deron sat motionless in disbelief. Vanessa came from the kitchen to bring Lawrence another drink, totally neglecting Deron's. She refused to even make eye contact. There was obvious tension between the two and even Lawrence felt it, but remained mum on that subject, at least until he had Deron alone.

"Yea man so that's the story." Lawrence said, breaking the silence.

"So what happened next? I mean how did they keep you alive for 20 something years while staying in that garbage can of a shed?" Deron asked as he stood and walked to the kitchen, right past Vanessa to get himself another drink. He came back and before sitting, he tapped Lawrence's bottle with his as if to say "Cheers."

"Deron, all I know man, is that it's by the grace of God that I'm sitting here talking to you. They did horrible things to me and thinking back, its damn near miraculous that I'm here man." Lawrence said taking a drink of his beer.

"What kind of things did they do to you and why do you think they chose you?" Deron asked inquisitively.

"Well that's still to be determined, but you name it and they did it. They pissed on me, spit on me and beat me senseless many times. They kept me in that shed the whole time. They placed me where there was a leak in the roof. Each time it rained, I got drenched. I can laugh about it now,

but they told me when it rained, that was my shower."
Lawrence said stretched out in the recliner holding his drink
in one hand and the other positioned behind his head.

Deron sat there amazed that a man was held captive for
almost 25 years and was being tortured still had the strength
to praise God.

"Deron man, there are a lot of things I don't even wanna
think about ya know. Things I don't wanna relive."

"Yea I understand."

"No. Deron you don't understand, trust me, you have
no clue. I just owe whatever life I have left on this world to
you for getting me out of there." Lawrence said as he turned
to face Deron.

"Man, don't mention it." Deron said as they clanged
beer bottles again.

"So what's the plan now Lawrence?"

"Now I find my family. Well my wife and daughter
because other than those two, I didn't have much of a family.
They were all the family I needed."

"So give me some info on them man, damn." Deron
joked.

"My wife's name is Edna, Edna Silverman and my
daughter's name is Zoe Silverman. I miss my baby so much
man. She had big puffy cheeks, curly hair and the biggest,
cutest hazel eyes you would ever see. She was always smiling
and she was a little dark baby." Lawrence said and the more
he thought about his baby girl, the more tears pushed
themselves out of his eyes.

"My wife and I were having problems at the time so we
were a little like you and Vanessa now." Lawrence whispered.

"Man what you talking 'bout, we good." Deron said in
denial.

"Deron y'all ain't good, I know good when I see it and
y'all ain't that." Lawrence said while laughing.

"Whatever, why were you and your wife having

problems?" Deron asked as he sipped from his bottle, taking a big gulp.

"Well, I was away a lot on the road. I was a truck driver, but a local one. She didn't like my job, but it paid the bills ya know. She always wanted more than what we had because she was materialistic and had fancy taste. Another thing I didn't like was how she treated our daughter man. She had no connection with her, I was the one that played with her. I was the one that fed her, I was the one that changed her and put her to bed. My wife had no connection with our daughter whatsoever and that always bothered me and it began to affect our marriage." Lawrence said while finishing off his warm drink.

"Damn man that's messed up. Sorry to hear that. So, how old was your daughter when you were taken away?" Deron asked

"She was 3. Three years old man and she's 24, about your age now." Lawrence said as his head dropped.

"Come on man, we're gonna find them ok, just be careful. I have a tendency to see the future and I may end up dating your daughter. I'm a smooth guy." Both men laughed hysterically. Deron popped up and hit Lawrence on the leg, telling him to get up.

"Get up man, let's go to the store." Deron said as he grabbed his keys and left without letting Vanessa know where they were headed.

Deron and Lawrence were at Jerry's Super Market waiting in the long express line. Deron was talking, but had no idea nobody was listening. Lawrence saw something that made him as still as a deer caught in headlights.

"Lawrence!" Deron yelled.

"Lawrence! Man what are you looking at?" Deron screamed to get Lawrence's attention.

"Deron?" Lawrence stood still, his eyes were focused on something and no parts of him moved.

"Man what is it?" Deron questioned.

"That's her." Lawrence said in a subdued tone. There was a gorgeous woman wearing black and grey furry snow boots and fitted dark jeans with along fitting pink winter sweater.

She was light skinned, had full lips and a great smile, and her eyes were hazel. Her eyebrows were perfectly arched and her eyelashes were long and finely curled. Lawrence zeroed in on her, but he was stuck in his stance. His feet were firmly planted to the cold tile floor.

"What man, you like her or something?" Deron asked while he leaned on his cart full of groceries. Lawrence didn't answer nor did he blink when Deron snapped his fingers in front of his eyes.

"Deron, that's her! That's my wife." Lawrence said. He froze like he saw a ghost.

"Well, what the hell are you waiting on? Go talk to her."

Deron said as he gave Lawrence a shove and he took a few steps as if he was learning to walk again. A tall handsome man walked up to the lady and grabbed her hand. As soon as he did, Lawrence froze and turned his back to the couple.

"Deron we have to go right now! Right now!" Lawrence screamed tight lipped.

"Deron, leave that shit here, we have to go, I will explain later. Let's go!" Lawrence screamed again.

Finally, they made it home and Lawrence was quiet the entire ride. As soon as Deron opened the door he asked Lawrence what was going on. He started reading a letter laid out on the glass coffee table from Vanessa. Deron stared at it for awhile, smacked his teeth and balled the letter up. After brought the groceries inside, Deron asked Lawrence again.

"Man what the hell happened back there?" Lawrence stayed silent, his hands shook and he was rocking back and forth on the edge of the recliner.

"Lawrence man, talk to me." Deron begged. Lawrence began to hit himself repeatedly in the face and then his head. He couldn't stop his cries.

"Deron, we need to find my daughter you hear me? We need to find her!" Lawrence screamed.

"Ok Lawrence, we will, but is there any particular reason why you say that now?" Deron asked nervously.

"Deron, that man that was with my wife, he….he was…" Lawrence cried and stuttered.

"Lawrence, he was what?" Deron asked slowly as he sat at the edge of the couch.

"Deron, he was the cop that did that shit to me. He's the cop Deron. My wife, ex wife or widow, I don't know, but whatever she is, she's married to the man that did all of this shit to me."

"Lawrence, let's go to New York." Deron said as he slammed back against the couch.

"What? Go to New York? After I just told you that shit?" Lawrence screamed. He stood up and headed to the door as if he was about to leave, but Deron stopped him and showed him the balled up letter.

"Look at this. This is a letter from Vanessa saying she left me. This is my chance to go find my Janiya and help you out at the same time. Look, we won't be able to do anything for you here in Texas. All of these cops know about you and we won't be able to get anywhere with them when it comes to you. Let's go to New York to help both of our situations out." Deron explained.

"Deron did you say Janiya?" Lawrence asked.

"Yea Janiya, why?"

"My wife always wanted to name our daughter Janiya. Her middle name is Jae, but Edna always called her Janiya. That's funny huh?" Lawrence sarcastically smiled.

"Yea yea, funny. Are you in, or out?" Deron asked.

Lawrence had no choice. He was in. While Deron packed his clothes, he told Lawrence the whole story between him and Janiya. Lawrence fully understood why there was no fight in Deron to keep Vanessa. She was holding him back from finding the other half of his heart.

CHAPTER 20

2001

What better way could a beautiful hard working woman like Janiya spend her day than in the most popular diner in town? Giovanni's Breakfast and Lunch Diner was definitely a tourist attraction and it was located right in the heart of the city of Brooklyn, NY, where Janiya now lived.

She had come a long way since the dark and scary days of living at home and dealing with her parents. She still has yet to talk to either one of them since the day she walked out the door of Phillip's fancy home.

Janiya graduated at the age of 17 and finished law school at the tender age of 24. She busted her ass to build the reputation she had. She worked endlessly and had an unmatched work ethic. She was determined to be the best and she was. She was now a very successful attorney at the age of 25. She worked so hard that she became one of the youngest women ever to have her own firm.

Going through the phase of dealing with Rob, she

thought it was time to stop feeling bad and get on with her life.

Janiya came home to a trashy apartment. Clothes were thrown all over the floor. Dirty pots and pans rested on her stove and cold cuts wrappings were laid on her counter. There were traces of Rob making him something to eat. He never cleaned after himself and that grew old with Janiya.

She continued to walk in her small rubbishy apartment, stepping over any and everything. There were knocked over lamps, old books and torn up coloring book pages from when Rob's daughter would come to visit.

Janiya slowly walked towards her bedroom, tossing her leather Coach purse on the crowded dinner table. Approaching the door, she heard the sounds of Rob enjoying some pleasure that she obviously couldn't provide.

She tiptoed away from the door with a sly sarcastic smile on her face and she quietly opened her coat closet to grab her friend out of there. A shiny .357 magnum was Janiya's new best friend.

She kissed it and loaded it before heading back to the room. Listening in one more time, Janiya shook her head and slowly opened the door only to find Rob receiving oral treatment from a big heavy set man, also with cornrows.

Rob was laid out on the cluttered bed. One hand at the rear of his head and the other hand directing the gigantic, shadow colored man's head.

Janiya once again smiled sarcastically, yet quietly as she watched the joyous and pleased expressions on Rob's face. She no longer felt bad about Rob finishing the job himself in her bathroom after they had sex. At that moment, that instant of watching Rob's face of sheer enjoyment and satisfaction, she realized that she didn't have the necessary tools to completely satisfy him.

It was a relief to Janiya because after being raped repeatedly by Phillip, she began to believe everything he had ever told her about how nobody would ever want her and how nobody would ever need her or love her because of what he did to her.

Janiya had began to believe that she was incapable of ever pleasing a man, but she felt a huge load being lifted off of her shoulders. She just stood there watching until she finally tapped on the door with gun.

"Good evening boys, are you guys having fun?" Janiya said. The corner of her mouth was turned up and she leaned her head against the door while Rob and his male lover frantically jumped up.

"Oh shit, baby, baby it ain't what you think ok." Rob said, shoving his dick back into his pants. The big, black monster, the nickname Janiya had so cleverly given him, pulled the covers up to his face.

"It's not what I think? What is it then? Because it looks like you are getting head from this big black, gay ass monster. It's ok tho' baby. Really it is." Janiya said still tapping her shiny powerful best friend against the door.

"It's ok Rob, all I will say is you and your little friend there get out of my house please? Ok?"

"Baby wait…." Rob screamed, but Janiya interrupted.

"Now see, you're not following directions sweetie. Trust me, I'm not mad…yet. Just do what I say. You and your little friend get out of my house before my finger really starts to make love to this trigger. You don't have to understand, because I can painfully see that I never had the tools or the attachments to satisfy you Rob" Janiya said while smiling.

"I'm gonna count to 3 and if you muthafuckas aint heading out that door, I will start shooting!" Janiya screamed. She no longer had a sly grin on her face.

That day was the last time Janiya had seen or heard of Rob. She made sure to throw everything he had in her apartment away. The same day she cleaned up her house, looked herself in the mirror and decided she didn't like who she had become. Janiya vowed to change everything about herself and get back on track.

It was a rainy Friday evening and Janiya made up her mind. It was her first real day off in weeks and she wanted to go to her favorite diner for some coffee and a good a read. She sashayed her way in and was excited when she saw that her favorite seat was open, but was disappointed when she found out that a gay guy was sitting pretty close to her table.

Janiya usually didn't have a problem with gay guys, but when the whole Rob situation happened, she had a new evil vision toward gays.

It was just off in a quiet corner with windows behind her and on the side of her. Janiya loved to read. She also enjoyed looking outside at the people living their lives. What pissed her off was seeing couples walking hand and hand expressing their love. It was somewhat understandable to Janiya, but no woman would want to see love when love constantly ran away from them.

Actually, since Deron many years ago, Janiya never really got close enough to love for it to run away so she was content with pulling six figures a year and working her ass off.

While taking a break from her book, Janiya glanced outside and saw a handsome young man making his way into the diner. She definitely liked what she saw, a nice looking black man with a suit on.

Janiya just loved a man in a suit. She especially liked what she saw about this man. She watched the way he moved and wasn't thrilled about his walk, but she couldn't take her eyes off him.

She sort of felt cheated. Here was a man that seemed to

be the total package physically. He was a tall, dark and handsome man who definitely knew how to dress. She wondered why a lack of confidence showed in his walk. Although he stuck his chest out, his shoulders slumped and his head hung low instead of high with swagger. Janiya watched and noticed he was a self foot watcher, meaning his eyes looked down instead of out in front of him.

Janiya sat there still thinking about how gorgeous this man was and the weird walk he had. He disappeared and appeared inside of the diner. Finally, his eyes looked up and Janiya caught a glimpse of him looking right at her. She looked him over and gave a pretty inviting smile.

Janiya began to pretend like she was really reading her book; she clutched her coffee with one hand, danced her hanging hair behind her ear and took a sip as she felt him walk up.

"Hello, are you sitting alone?" This tall, russet skinned man said as he came to introduce himself. Janiya thought to herself 'Damn this brother is fine'. He had a tantalizing smile and was clean cut. He wore a very nice Armani suit, had well manicured fingernails and there was no wedding ring.

"Yes I am." Janiya replied with a subtle, and hidden excited tone.

"My name is Chris, Chris Williamson and you are?" He asked as he held out his hand and just as he did, Janiya caught a whiff of his cologne. 'Damn this man even smell good', she thought to herself. His hands were huge and there Janiya sat gazing at them thinking about his strong hands maneuvering all over her body. Quickly she snapped out of it and shook his hand.

"Hi Chris, my name is Janiya, Janiya Brakens."

"That's a lovely name for a lovely woman. Would you mind if I sat down and joined you Janiya?"

"Well, that depends on why you want to sit with me Chris." She could tell that she caught him off guard. His eyebrows quickly jumped up and his smile slightly went away.

Janiya was a strong minded black woman that has been through hell and back a few times. She also has put a few men through hell herself. From a man's point of view, Janiya was everything they could ever want, she was breath taking. Janiya stood 5'7 with caramel skin made just for all 5 senses.

She worked out tirelessly after ridding herself of the cancerous Rob. She now had the body that many women would kill for and every time she wore her heels, her calves screamed out "yea I'm the shit." As astounding as Janiya was, life for her had been traumatic and she had no problem telling her story to people.

"Well, Janiya, I saw you sitting here alone and I thought to myself that you were too pleasing to the eye to be sitting alone."

"Well Chris, what is it that you really want?" Janiya said as she sat back in her chair while kicking her heels up and down. Chris's eyes squinted in shock, and his shoulders were thrown back as he started rubbing the thin hairs in his goatee.

"What does that mean? I just want to get to know you, that's all." Chris replied.

"Come on now Chris, all men want something and I'm giving you an opportunity to tell me what it is you want. Here's your chance to be completely honest." Janiya said with a grin painted on her face. The dent in her dimples told Chris that she was having fun with him, but serious at the same time.

"Look Janiya, to be straight up with you, I'm just trying to get to know you. I never understood the question of 'what is it that you really want'. Regardless of the men that you have come across, this man in front of you needs to get to know you before I can even want anything." Chris said he took a sip of his raspberry lemonade and looked directly in Janiya's eyes.

She looked Chris up and down desperately trying to find

his angle. Even though she was angered by Chris's tone, she was also turned on at the same time. Janiya's garden moistened at the thought of a man controlling her and the situation with honesty.

She knew that she had dwelled in her somber solitude for far too long. Trusting a man was something she couldn't fathom ever doing again unless it was Deron. Janiya sat there clutching her coffee with both hands as Chris watched her. There was a heavy intense argument going on in her head about whether or not to open up to this man.

Chris interrupted Janiya's thinking by saying "I'll help you out. What do you do for a living?"
Janiya showed her toothy smile. She appreciated the absence of the normal first question from men 'hey, you got a man'. She slid the hair hanging in front of her face behind her ear. She sat her coffee down and finally gave in.

"Well, I work for a very successful law firm called Brakens & Associates Family Law." Janiya said as she lifted her glasses that were hung on the tip of her nose.

"Wow! Brakens & Associates Family Law huh? So when you say 'work for' you mean....." Chris asked as he cleared his throat and desperately trying his best to paint an excited look on his face.

"Yea I work for them.....and sort of...It's my practice. Why do you seem so shocked?" Janiya finally blurted out and followed with a sarcastic laugh.

"That's great! Wow! I knew you did more than just work there, hence the name." Chris replied while as he reached for his drink again.

"Why do you seem so surprised? Also, what do you do for a living?"

"I know I'm not the first person that has reacted this way when you told them that you have your own law firm. I wouldn't say I'm surprised. You look like a very successful young lady. It's just that I wasn't expecting you to say you have your own law firm. That's great. As for me, I am a Pastor in a church in Colleyville and I'm an interior designer."

"Oh ok." replied Janiya as signals suddenly crossed her mind. Manicured nails, fancy top of the line clothing, clean cut, perfectly trimmed eye brows, what else was a girl to think?

"Just ok?" Chris asked.

"Yea, just a lot of things running through my mind. Anyway, what got you into Interior design?" Janiya asked as she tried in vain to distract the thoughts in her mind.

"I like fashion and I like things to look good. When I was little, my mom always wanted my opinion on how to decorate something or what she looked good in. She knew I had good taste. Now, let's get back to what's going on in your head." Chris said while his voice was getting higher and higher.

"Calm down Chris, it's nothing." Janiya sensed some frustration and picked up some more worrisome hints. There was an eerie silence between the two as Janiya tapped her fingers on her coffee mug. Her eyes were wandering around and Chris wiped lent off of his suit while finishing off his lemonade.

"Chris?" Janiya called out while her head hung low down.

"Yes Janiya?"

"Are you gay?" Janiya finally blurted out. Chris sat there motionless.

"Well you obviously think I am, so why don't you tell me why you think I am Janiya." Chris replied as he sat back shaking his glass to the waitress, signaling for another drink.

Janiya sat there with the most innocent smile drawn on her face. She knew what she had been through and wanted to know up front what she was dealing with.

She did recognize the sensitivity of the subject and she knew exactly how she attacked Chris's ego, but a part of her no longer cared. Janiya had been through hell with men. She pretty much resided there and she has no plans to ever return to that low place.

Even though Janiya could see something in Chris's eyes that was different, the warning signs still remained. She would not let herself succumb to the idea of not inquiring about it.

She'd given all she had and was emotionally battered. She told herself to trust someone one last time. She was not about to go through the same that she went through with Rob. She didn't want the surprise of a gay man again.

"I don't think you are Chris, but I read somewhere that more than 3 million women are, or have been wives or girlfriends of men who secretly had sex with other men. Do you know how severe that is Chris? Knowing this, would you look for signals too? If you were a woman of course? It's not really a big deal to you men because if your woman was secretly having sex with another woman, you men would say 'baby all you had to do was tell me and we all could have had some fun'. So can you see why this is a sensitive subject for women? I know this is kind of deep for a first conversation, but if you only knew my past. It's like you said earlier. I'm trying to get to know you and I've been through the whole "down low brother" thing. I have no plans of playing that all boys game again." Janiya said. A laugh followed, but wasn't returned.

"Excuse me if I'm a little out of line, but with you being a lawyer, I'm very surprised that you are judging a book by its cover."

"Well Chris, my life experiences come before what I do professionally and if you knew my life and my past, you would understand that. I do not live my profession 24 hours a day and, believe it or not, everyone judges. I simply go based on signals." Janiya said as she whipped her hair back behind her shoulders.

"And what signals are those Miss Michaels? If you don't mind me asking." Chris said. A smile finally appeared sarcastically on his face. His eyes lived on Janiya, never breaking away from her. It was obvious that Janiya irritated Chris, but there was something interesting about her that made him not get completely angered by her accusations.

"Come on, Chris don't use that tone. You know we all go on signals. I'm sure read you my signals before you came over here to introduce yourself. There was something about me that triggered you to come over. Obviously I didn't give off a 'fuck off' signal or you wouldn't have come, right?" Janiya said leaning back in her chair.

He sat there in silence because a part of him knew she had a point. He saw a good-looking woman with her hair tied back in a ponytail with a few strands hanging down in front of her eyes. He saw a woman that possessed the most dazzling smile to him. He had stood in line to order lemonade and never took his eyes off the Janiya. Finally, their eyes met and Chris fell inside Janiya's deep dimples as she smiled at him and continued to sip her coffee and read her book.

"You are right and wrong. We all judge, but there is an unintentional judgment and intentional judgment. I'm still waiting on you to tell me the signals I somehow gave off that made you question my sexuality." Chris said as he leaned in closer so no one would over hear the conversation.

"You mean the signals that made me question your sexuality and the question you still haven't answered yet?" Janiya replied. She knew that statement would probably piss him off and she wouldn't blame him if he got up and walked away, but a part of her hoped he wouldn't.

His fingers tapped slowly on the table. They began to tap faster and faster. He no longer kept his eyes on Janiya. Instead, he looked around the diner and sat back in his seat as if he was trying to calm himself down.

"I can't believe that instead of asking you your hobbies, if you have kids, or what do you do for fun, I'm defending my sexuality, wow. Can you please just tell me what signals you are referring to so I can answer them and we can finally move on to something else?" Janiya smacked her lips at Chris's remarks.

Again, she had mixed feelings. Here was a man attempting to control her by making demanding statements. He did so in sexy way that turned her on. Janiya finally became submissive to Chris's questions.

"Fine Chris. When I saw you, I saw perfectly shaped eyebrows. They look like you go and get them arched. Your fingers are not only are clean, but they look better than man. There is not a hair out of place on you and it just seems that everything about you is done with such precision. Also, there's your walk, it doesn't really scream 'I'm a straight man'. Then there was that glance at the man sitting across from us. He's obviously gay, and I saw the eye contact between you two. I'm not saying that you are gay, but if you are its cool, just let me know so I'll know what I'm dealing with. That's all I'm saying." Janiya took a deep breath and her eyes apologized to Chris. She was sorry, but was too proud to say it herself.

Janiya sat there patiently waiting on a reaction from Chris. A part of her really liked him. She liked that he seemed to possess a calm control about himself.

Janiya had her own family law practice and very successful at it. In fact, her practice was the number one in Brooklyn. She was pretty much accustomed to being in charge and basically had people kiss her ass. She somewhat enjoyed it, but she always liked when a man could control her. She knew how hard she made it for men.

Janiya was a woman who spoke freely. If people hated the things that came out of her mouth, then they would want no parts of knowing what she was thinking. She felt bad for certain things that she said, but it would never stop her from speaking her mind.

"So, a man can't get groomed without someone thinking he's gay? Instead of going back and forth, I'll just say I'm not gay and end it there. I know what I am and what I'm not and I'm not really into defending something based on someone's judgment of me." Chris said with a serious tone.

"What do you think about me, now that you have gotten to know me?" Janiya said. She smiled and held a pencil up to her dimple.

"Well, I think you are a very lovely woman and have a delightful smile that can light up any man's heart. It shows that you take care of your body very well. Before you ask, I am complimenting your physical appearance first because as much as we talked Janiya, I still have yet to really get to know you. I mean, we spent a plethora of time talking about you passing judgment on the signals you got instead of really getting to know me. I definitely still want to get to know you." Chris said softly.

His eyes were once again painted on Janiya's face. He was serious and determined to get what he wanted, and that was to get to know Janiya.

"Well sadly, signals have become a woman's confirmation. If I would have paid attention to certain signals, I may be better off." Janiya said as her eyes slowly dropped.

"I have really enjoyed my talk with you and I hope I haven't pissed you off totally." Janiya said as she laughed, hoping Chris would return the laugh this time.

"Janiya, women don't scare me. Even battered women do not scare me. You are a woman that's obviously been through some things and if that scared me, I can plan to be single for a very long time." They both laughed as Chris stood and held out his hand.

Janiya reached in her purse and pulled out her card with

her number on it. She hesitated for a moment. She thought about every situation she had been through and realized that giving Chris her number would mean she trusts someone again. She wasn't sure if she could do that so soon or even at all.

"Here's my number Chris. I hope you plan to use it." Janiya said with a hint of indecisiveness in her voice.

"I enjoyed my talk with you as well Janiya. I definitely look forward to talking to you and getting to know more about you." Janiya smiled and walked away, she looked back at Chris and he had the hugest smile on his face.

She thought to herself 'he watching my ass', that's a good sign. As Janiya walked off, she noticed the gay guy next to her table looking at Chris.

CHAPTER 21

The summer for Janiya had been the best she had ever experienced. There wasn't a day that went by that she didn't crave Chris. It wasn't because of the way he made her feel physically, but more so mentally. If fact, in the five months they've known each other, Janiya still had reservations about fully opening herself up to him physically.

She enjoyed their cuddle time together and she loved that Chris was incredibly intimate with her, but her past constantly haunted her every chance she thought about giving in. Chris and Janiya went on long walks in the park and enjoyed each other's company during picnics. Janiya really loved that because it allowed her to be out in nature and be comfortable lying on Chris's hard, strong body.

Her favorite nights with Chris were when they would go to Eleanor's, a jazz night club right in the middle of Brooklyn. Secretly, Janiya loved to go Eleanor's because it reminded her of Deron and the way he spoke. Deron had always stayed in the heart of Janiya. He never left since the day she looked up at her window that rainy night. Lorretta broke both of their hearts by taking him home.

The way he talked to her, the way he looked at her, and the way he touched her that night, she knew she was in love.

Without knowing it, any man that entered her life had to live up to the touch and sight of Deron.

Chris was the only man that came remotely close to matching the feeling she got when she thought of Deron. He was the only man other than Deron, to ever hold her the way she wanted and when she wanted. It took her a long time to even allow him to do that.

Her heart was no longer the same, no longer pure and innocent as it was when she first talked to Deron. Being raped over and over definitely brought issues that had followed Janiya wherever she went and with whomever she decided to be intimate with. The relationship she had with Rob was an obvious case of low self esteem that was also brought on because of her events with Philip.

Janiya laid in her king size bed alone. She was tossing and turning with little to nothing on, which was the way she loved to sleep. For a long time she slept with layers and layers of clothes on. Shorts, long johns and pajama pants would straddle her lower half while a tank top, tee shirt or long john top straddled her top half. She had been subconscious of her body and what had been done to it, until, with the help of time, finally got out of that phase. She was planted in her bed with a black laced bra and panties. Her body was scorching hot.

Janiya imagined Chris's beautiful sculpted body lying next to her. She imagined him touching her, kissing her and making love to her. Images of her kissing his rock hard abs with her full pouty lips ran repeatedly through her mind. She daydreamed about overlapping Chris's body while she moaned in ecstasy. She saw visions of herself in the mirror as Chris made love to her in different positions. As images and thoughts filled her mind, Janiya's legs moved vehemently across her bed until she couldn't take it anymore.

Janiya turned over and saw her clock. It read 3:38 am. She decided at that moment, the time had finally come. She would let go of all of the hurt, all of the pain that she's been through and finally give in to her desires to be with Chris. She called Chris and as soon as she heard his deep, sexy voice, she smiled innocently.

"Hello." Chris answered.

"Hey baby."

"Sup beautiful." Chris responded with a grungy tone.

"I know you're sleep baby so I'll make this short and sweet. You should come over." Janiya said with the softest and sexiest voice she could make.

"When? Now?" Chris asked excitingly.

"No Chris, next week. Geez! Yes now!" Janiya said while laughing.

"Ahh baby, I'm sorry. I can't I have to go by the office in the morning for a meeting with a very important client." Chris said as he rolled over on his back. He was shirtless and he rubbed his smooth bare chest as he talked to Janiya.

"Can't you just leave from here in the morning Chris? You won't be sorry." Janiya said as she pouted.

"Baby you know if I came over, then there would be a good chance I would miss that meeting. I'm sorry baby." Chris said while sitting up in the bed. He took a sip of his warm water that he always kept on his nightstand.

"Ok, I guess." Janiya lip's turned upside down and her eyes drooped. Her once excited legs were now crossed over each other, still as a calm night.

"Don't be like that. How about I come over as soon as my meeting is over? Would that be ok?" Chris begged.

"Yes that's fine. I'll let you get back to sleep and I'll see you as soon as you get here. Goodnight." Janiya was upset, but not angry with Chris. His ambition and professionalism were a turn on to her.

Chris said his good bye and Janiya fluffed her pillow. She gave a quick thought about Deron and was off to sleep.

It was 11:00 AM, well passed Janiya's wake up time. She couldn't believe that she slept that late and she really couldn't believe that not one missed call from Chris showed on her phone.

She stepped out of her bed and took her cell phone off the charger. No text message notifications either. Janiya remembered Chris saying he had an important meeting, so if it was going on this long, that could only be good news, she thought.

She cleaned herself up, threw on her favorite shorts and tee shirt and decided to go ahead and prep the house for when Chris arrived. A rubber band dangled in her mouth as she tied her hair in a ponytail. Her phone rang.

"Hello."

"Babe?" Chris's voice excited Janiya and instantly. A smile formed her face.

"Baby, where are you?" Janiya screamed. Chris remained quiet for a few seconds.

"Janiya have you seen the news yet?" Chris asked.

"No. I just woke up, why? What happened now?" Janiya said as she rested the phone between her ear and her shoulder so she could multi-task.

"Can you go turn on the TV now Janiya, please?" Chris begged. He always had Janiya look at the news since he was a pastor. He wanted Janiya to see events on the news. He had to minister funerals from all of the murders in the area. So Janiya walked over and turned on the news.

"Ok baby, I have it on." She said as she sat down with the remote in her hand. The morning sun beamed in her eyes, but Janiya welcomed it to help wake her up.

"Ok, hold on, I'm flipping through the channels, but the same movie is on every channel. What channel do you want me to put it on baby?" Janiya asked.

"It doesn't matter."

"What do you mean?" Janiya continued to ask while she flipped through same channels, seeing the same movie on each one.

"Janiya, baby that ain't no movie." Chris said.

"Huh, what are you talking about?"

"Babe, do you see the planes going into the buildings?" Chris asked. Janiya's mouth opened wide as she couldn't believe what she was watching.

"Baby, where are you? Please tell me you are on your way here. Tell me that Chris!" Janiya cried as she continued to watch the footage of planes crashing into the World Trade Centers in New York.

"Chris, honey where are you?" Janiya cried out again.

"Baby... I'm still at the office. Do you understand what I'm telling you baby?" Chris cried.

"No! No! Chris don't you tell me that. You told me you were coming to see me, please Chris come see me. Please!" Janiya cried out at the top of her lungs.

"Babe, I love you." Chris cried.

"Baby, don't you tell me that right now. You just get out of there and come tell me that to my face." Janiya screamed. That was the first time she believed a man when he said he loved her. She was never sure if Deron loved her. She didn't have memories of her dad telling her that, but she was also too young to remember. Phillip definitely didn't tell her, nor did Rob.

"Janiya I can't. You've been to my office. You know what floor I'm on too. Baby we are stuck here with no way out." Chris voice began to tremble. He knew he had to face a decision that was not in his favor.

"Janiya, there's no way out. There's no way to get out of here. There's no way to the bottom floor. All of the elevators are down and the fires are here outside of our office. Babe we are stuck."

"Baby, you told me you were coming. That's what you told me. You told me you were coming."

"Janiya, baby I love you. Tell me you love me. I need to hear you tell me that." Chris cried.

"Come to me Chris and I will tell you. Let me tell you to your face." Janiya begged in denial.

"Janiya, baby you have to accept what's going on. What's about to happen. I've accepted God as my Lord and Savior. If this is His will, baby I can't fight it. I refuse to leave this earth without hearing you tell me you love me." Chris cried uncontrollably. He tried his best to remain calm, but he failed. Although, he was a strong believer in God and His plan, he was hurting and scared for Janiya.

Chris wondered what this would do to her, how this would set her back even more. That broke his heart more than leaving the world.

"Baby, what I need is for you not to talk like that. Just get your ass here. If you loved me like you said you do, then baby find your way out of there." Janiya pleaded. She heard a loud explosion in the background and a piercing scream rang through the phone and into Chris's ears.

"Baby! Baby! Baby!" Janiya continued to call for Chris.

"Sorry baby, the fire has broken down the doors. Baby people are starting to jump out of the window. Baby, tell me you love me. I need you to be strong."

"But…baby…." Janiya wept into the phone.

"No, Janiya, you will be ok. You have to accept what's happening. You will go on to be great. Just make sure you never forget me. Janiya, you will go on to marry a great man that will love you endlessly. You will marry him and you will have beautiful kids. Janiya I have to go, don't ever forget me." Chris' voice cracked and trembled. As strong as he was at that moment, or as strong as he tried to come across, Chris was scared of his decision.

"Baby..no no no...no no no, don't leave Chris, don't go. I love you, baby did you hear me? I said I love you, so you don't have to do this, I love you Chris." Janiya cried out as loud as she could.

"I love you too Janiya. Thank you." Chris said right before he hung up the phone and jumped out of the window, from the 90th floor. Janiya yelled out Chris's name repeatedly and slammed her phone down. She watched the news show people jumping out of the window.

Janiya cried miserably and wondered what she ever did to deserve the horrible things that had happened to her. She was in the fetal position crying uncontrollably. She now accepted the fact that Chris was gone.

CHAPTER 22

Deron and Lawrence had been in New York for almost a year now. They finally wrapped up the long investigation that led to Phillip being arrested and sentenced to life in prison. Many other officers were arrested as well for being co-conspirators. To Lawrence, it wasn't a complete satisfaction and it didn't take the pain or the events that he suffered away, but now his mind was clear from worrying if he would ever go back.

Both had come to the decision that they would split up since the investigation was done. Deron would stay in New York to continue to look for Janiya and Lawrence would go back to Dallas to try and find his daughter.

Lawrence wanted to celebrate his last night in New York by listening to Deron recite some of his work at their favorite jazz spot, Eleanor's, in Brooklyn. It was a rainy night and just seemed to portray the perfect New York scene.

Rain, shiny lights, music, poetry and people were the perfect atmosphere for Janiya to get out and get her mind off of her tragic loss. She sat in a dark and quiet nook in the corner of the club with a perfect view of the club.

Janiya had gotten out of her recent norm of wearing all black every place she went. She finally decided to put on makeup and wear other colors that weren't the color of death. She wore orange knee high boots and an orange skirt with a tan sweater. Initially she wanted to wear her hair long and straight. If she had stayed home to straighten it, she would have changed her mind about going. She left it long, shiny and wavy.

Shortly after she arrived, she left to go to the ladies room to cry again. She found herself randomly doing that and she hated it and loved it at the same time. As she dabbed her eyes with the soggy Kleenex, she prayed to God that he would release the pain from her heart and let her live peacefully from this moment on.

Janiya sashayed her way back to her seat and there was a gentleman already up reciting his work. She ordered another drink with the waitress and forced a smile on her face so she could at least look like her prayers were being answered. The next poet was up.

Deron slowly walked up to the stage. His brown Kangol hat hung just over the shades that covered his nervous eyes. In one hand, Deron had a small glass of Brandy and he sipped slowly before he began. It traveled smoothly through his body as he grabbed the mic.

"Hey love, can I be your music tonight? Can I rhythm and blues my way inside you and enjoy your lyrics of mmm's and ahh's baby? Can my love instrument play alongside your orchestra and make smooth melodies of moans. Enjoy the concert I give while I'm performing a tasteful soul love ballad inside your…." Deron paused and backed away from the mic while moaning. Lawrence sat at table near the stage and he snapped his fingers along with the other onlookers.

Janiya felt herself getting wrapped up with the words she was hearing. Something about the words made her tingle in way it hadn't in a long time. Deron continued.

"Through the rhythm of your mmm's and the blues in your ahh's, my hands indented themselves onto your thighs. My nature parted through remnants of your soul and into your heavens and earths, while love colored moans escaped your breath. Passion tears hung from your eyelids and your juices made for one hell of an adult beverage that I couldn't pass up."

Deron sipped his Brandy again to enhance the feeling of that last line.

"I drank from your well and became intoxicated instantly. I was sobered through the rhythm of your mmm's and the blues in your ahh's. Once there was a question, 'How many licks does it take to get to the center?' now I ask how many licks could your center take from the source that produces my dialect. My tongue that is, my tongue that is dripping with the essence of your presence, leaking with the quintessence of your... mmmm, dayum baby. My main vein anticipates flooding your center with a creamy decadence that would allow you to formulate the question 'How many licks does it take?' Once there was a question, 'How many licks does it takes to get to the center?' now I ask how many licks does it take for my tongue to enjoy the vernacular it and your center speak. How many licks does it take for me to taste you endlessly, splendidly, marvelously, superbly, magnificently and any other 'ly's? Could it be that the question meant the center of your heart darling? Sure, and I shall searcheth to the endeth of time until I find your center, grasp and orgasm your center, taste and love your center. Once there was a question, 'How many licks does it take to get to the center?' However many I can fit into a lifetime!"

The women melted as they snapped away. They kept asking for more and Deron glanced to the host to make sure that it was ok to keep going. After seeing the women in the club go crazy over his words, he waved at Deron as if to say, 'stay up there'.

Janiya found herself smiling and feeling a certain way that she hadn't felt since that morning she called Chris to invite him over. She squirmed in her seat and bit her lip more than she ever had before. The feeling she was feeling was much more intense.

It was more exciting and Janiya smiled as she sipped her strawberry margarita because she knew she didn't expect to feel the way this man had her feeling. Deron's deep voice continued to melt the hearts of all of the ladies in attendance and he asked if he could change things up and an explosion of yes's filled the room.

"On instinct, she arose from her bed only to find a body without a soul lying next to her. She spoke painfully without speaking from within and regretfully, she lived to love without ever loving. She thought to herself, how must one receive credit for existing in this world, rather living in it? Suddenly, her phone chirped and vibrated as a message from an unknown number came in."

Deron began to slowly walk off the stage with the mic in his hand. He walked by the women who held their begging hand out for Deron to touch. He made his way through the crowd and spotted an incredibly attractive woman in a quiet nook.

Finally, he stood inches away from Janiya, not knowing it was her and she not knowing it was him, because Deron's Kangol hat covered his face. Deron stood in front of Janiya and finished his story.

"It read, love, tear yourself away from yourself and sashay into my world of love. Remove the thoughts of anything prior to this message and come with me to gallop

blissfully into a world of climaxing passion, orgasmic loving and an everlasting overflow of mental stimulation. Depart from existing in the world that disappointed you and make a detour into a world that makes your velvety indulgence a desired taste. Report immediately into a world that allows your mind to become a piano, creating soothing music that warms the soul, stimulates goose bumps, soothes my.....soothes my.....ok where was I? Oh yea, soothes my nature as it prepares to seed your garden. Prance joyfully, willfully into my world as I will forever feast inside your lucky charms. Dance with me forever as we, cleverly make love while only looking and feeling inside of each other's heart. Take this message and meet me inside this world. Dive inside this world as I would soon enjoy the pleasures of deep sea diving inside, mmm, inside you. See you soon.
Love...Love... Love you know who. She followed directions and dove right away with no hesitation, no reservations. She dove inside love!

Janiya went crazy, her lips trembled, her hands shook and if her eyes could salivate, she would need to wipe them desperately. Other women screamed out that they would dive and many other women tugged at Deron as he made his way back to the stage.

"Thank you Brooklyn, that's my time and I'm truly happy you enjoyed my words. Before I leave, I would like to say a special good bye to my great friend down there. Lawrence, man we've been through a great deal and I'm excited for you. Lawrence has been through some things that no one would believe. We can finally talk about it now. Lawrence was taken away by the police over 20 years ago and held captive the entire time. He was taken away from his wife and taken away from his 3 year old daughter. Now that the investigation is over and all of the parties involved have been arrested, my friend is leaving. He's leaving while I stay here to look for my long lost love that I haven't seen in over

10 years. Lawrence, I just want to say, good luck and you know you have to come back once you find her" Deron began to tear up and a woman in the audience screamed out to him.

"What would you say to her if you found her? If you found the love of your life, what would you say to her?" The woman screamed in an attempt to get Deron to recite more words from his heart.

Deron smiled and repeated what the woman asked.

"What would I say? If I saw her right now? I would let her know that we are truly the design of a heart. We started out at a point. You went your way with your heart and I went mine. Eventually we made it around the curves and found each other, in love with one another, because we met in the middle of each other's heart. That's what I would say." Deron said as he melted the hearts of women.

"If you all don't mind, I've been carrying a letter from her for a few years now, and I would like to read it aloud to you." Deron began to read the letter and after he spoke the first two words, Janiya's mouth dropped and tears ran down her face. She shivered from the chills and her hand covered her heart as she tried to stop her heart from beating so hard. Janiya fanned herself as she listened.

Hi Deron, I can't believe I'm doing this. First off, how are you doing? Me, I'm doing pretty good, I guess. I miss you like crazy Deron. I miss your handsome face, your stunning eyes and your sexy smile. I remember the feeling I had when you touched me and wow, it's giving me chills now as I write this letter. I hope you still think of me and I hope you find yourself missing me as well. Oh, I talked to Layla and she told me what happened to your parents. I'm sorry and I wish I could have been there for you because I could only imagine what was going through your mind. I have no idea where you are Deron and its crazy, but I wish I could find you like you found me that day. That was the most romantic thing I've ever witnessed and it was the greatest night. Deron, if you're out there somewhere, please come and find me again. I'm not sure how I could miss someone so much, but it makes perfect sense that it's you that I miss this much. How could something so special, so wonderful, so longed for and so treasured, be on such an undeserving mind like mine? Deron I need you right now more than ever and there are things I need to tell you that I should've told you when I had to chance. So Deron, if love is really as powerful as people say, then please find me Deron. I love you.

Deron held the letter in his hand and tears began to run down his face.

He removed his hat and took his shades off. Deron began to cry on stage and sniffs rang out around the Eleanor's. Lawrence stood and walked on stage to console his friend.

Janiya was making her way to the stage and the walk seemed like it took forever, but she managed. She was finally on stage.

"Deron." Janiya said softly. Deron's eyes opened wide and his heart felt like drums were being beat. He saw his Janiya, his best friend, the love of his life and instantly he started again, but this time he spoke directly to Janiya, knowing it was here. He was shocked after realizing he just recited something to her.

"Janiya, is it possible to believe in something so much and dream about something so much that it bleeds from your soul? Janiya, I can't think of anything to do but constantly tell you that I love you. More than love could possibly love. I want to make your heart glow with love and passion for an eternity. I have searched and found love's heaven inside your essence and serenity and I will not, shall not let it waver in the spoils of solitude. You are my world and I never imagined missing someone as much as I've missed you. You are my everything and I can't believe I'm standing in front of you right now." Deron said while wiping the tears from Janiya's eyes.

Lawrence never took his eyes off of Janiya. He saw Janiya and saw his daughter in her. He took the mic from Deron.

"Deron?" Lawrence tapped Deron on the shoulder and the people in the audience just sat there, not believing the miracle they were witnessing.

"Deron? Do you remember the day at your house when you told me to be careful because you would end up dating my daughter?" Lawrence asked while looking down. He spoke in a subdued tone and his hands held on to the microphone nervously.

"Yea Lawrence, I remember, I guess that won't happen now." Deron smiled, but Lawrence never returned the smile.

"Well Deron, that's my daughter right there." Lawrence said as he finally looked up. The once quiet nightclub, gasp loudly as the women whipped out the Kleenex again and wondered what was about to happen.

"What!" Deron screamed. Janiya stood there, motionless in the arms of Deron.

"That's not possible. My dad was killed in a car accident by a drunk driver when I was....." Lawrence interrupted Janiya.

"Let me guess, when you were 3." Lawrence said. Janiya covered her mouth once again.

"Yes, how did you know that?" Janiya asked.

"When you were 3, I was kidnapped by 2 officers and one being an Officer Phillip Brakens. He was your stepfather right?" Janiya began walking away backwards, crying uncontrollably and Deron was walking with her, not letting her go.

"Yes, he was the officer that came to our house to tell us you died in a car accident and shortly after mother married him and we moved into this big house."

"Deron, I have something else to say and I'm sorry, but her name isn't Janiya. Her birth name is Zoe Jae Silverman." Lawrence said and it was dead quiet on the stage. In classic fashion, Deron broke the silence.

"Well, I guess I was right! I told you to be careful because I could end up dating your daughter." Janiya sniffed and laughed simultaneously. She slowly walked away from Deron and ran to her dad. They embraced and held each other for what seemed like forever. Deron had his love, Janiya had her love and Lawrence had his daughter. It was a magical night in Brooklyn and Janiya remembered her prayer in the ladies bathroom as they all walked off of the stage. Her prayers came true.

CHAPTER 23

Many years had passed after that special night in Brooklyn, NY. Lawrence never returned back to Texas. They all stayed there in Brooklyn since it was so special to all of them. They all stayed together until Lawrence passed away 20 years after being reunited with Zoe.

After the confirmation came that Lawrence was indeed Zoe's father, she changed her name legally to Zoe Jae Silverman. After she'd done so, she had to change it again when her and Deron had gotten married. She was now Zoe Jae Jamison.

The couple went on to have 4 children, 3 girls and 1 boy with the boy being the youngest. Deron went on to write many books, but his most successful one was titled "Design of Their Heart" The story of he and Zoe's journey, it was a best seller and eventually a number 1 grossing movie that he helped write and direct.

They were married 47 years when Deron was diagnosed with cancer. It traveled fast and he had a short time to live. He and Zoe spent every day together and never left each other's side.

Deron laid there on his death bed still full of life and laughter, much more than his family had sitting beside him.

His daughter's sat around him numb to the moment and Zoe laid beside him in the bed, holding onto his frail body.

Deron let out slow dry coughs. With each cough and grasp for air, they knew the time was coming as did Deron, but still a smile was planted upon his pale face. His once strong and powerful hands were now thin and wrinkled. Gray hairs had withered away. They saw his weak and thin frame, but still saw their strong father. He was just less than what they were used to and it broke their hearts more than anything.

Deron was the strong, super dad that did it all, played sports and always won. He was always the strongest and to see him now hurt their hearts. Zoe didn't see it that way. She continued to see him as the strong man that she married. His physical stature never defined his strength to her, his faith, his belief and his love for her and his family is what made, and makes, him strong to her.

Deron Jr. stood against the wall off in the distance. He couldn't believe his father continued to smile. In a subdued tone, Deron Jr. began to speak.

"Dad, why must you smile?" Deron Jr. asked. With a smile that seemed to have an everlasting glow he said.

"Son, always remember this. When you see your queen, you smile. When you see your prince and princesses, you smile and when it's your time to see your king of kings, son, you smile." Deron smiled and Deron Jr. walked closer to his dad and hugged him.

"Baby?" Deron coughed.

"Yes honey?" Zoe whispered in his ear.

"I think it's time." Deron whispered back.

"Remember me and I will come back for you ok. No matter what happens. I will come back to you, exactly 12 years from now, on this day. Do you believe in love baby?" Deron asked while he coughed.

"Baby, I believe in you. If you tell me you will come get me, I'll be ready." Zoe whispered into his ear as Deron took his last breath.

Everyone cried except for Zoe. She remembered everything they had been through. How could she cry after looking at the life they built when times looked as if they would never see each other?

Zoe thought about one instance in particular. It was the day she told Deron about Phillip raping her and her mom knowing about it. His simple response was "I love you." Those three words from the perfect person released all of that pain from her heart and her mind.

Zoe smiled as she kissed him on his forehead and their children all followed her actions. They kissed him goodbye and walked out of the room, all crying again, except for Zoe.

It was the 12 year anniversary of Deron's passing and Zoe was now in a nursing home with Alzheimer's. The 85 year old Zoe woke up excited one morning. She was more excited than she had been in months. She walked around the nursing home telling anyone that would listen that Mr. Jamison was coming to get her today and that she haven't seen him in years.

No one had the heart to tell her that Mr. Jamison passed away 12 years ago.

"Mr. Jamison is coming to get me!" Zoe screamed again.

"And I'm going to light candles of his favorite scent which is Stormy Blue and I'm going to wear his favorite dress." She told everyone and they all nodded thinking she was crazy and didn't know what she was saying. What they didn't realize, when you believe in the power of love and you believe strongly in the one you love, you hang on to their every word. Zoe had done that when Deron told her 12 years ago, he would come back for her.

Before Zoe went to bed that night, she lit the candles and played music while wearing Deron's favorite dress.

Miraculously, all of the nurses got word that Zoe had passed away in her sleep and there was a note placed on Zoe's heart. Now today, that letter is the most famous letter around.

"My child, I saw how you looked at my queen when she told you I was coming. Well I in fact did come and she wore my favorite dress and we danced all night long. I told her I was coming and I came. I recited poetry to her while the music you hear now played in the background and she loved it so I will share it with you."

Torey Irving

I've searched for you
I have plowed through the rubble for you and have scarred
my hands
Searched through embers of past fires
So I can put together hopes of rekindling flames of passion
I have wandered hopefully, wishfully into the darkness in
search for you
And I have yet to see you, feel you, hear you, smell you, or
taste you
I have exhausted all of the possible possibilities of ever
having you
But not the ability to believe that I will, I will, I will have you
I will continue to plow through the rubble for you
And continue to scar my hands in search of you
I have no problems still searching through embers of past
fires
In hopes of rekindling flames of the once inevitable passion
I will continue to search for you, I will continue to love the
thought of loving you until I can say that I do love
Shit, I do love you. Shit, I love you
I now see I have searched for the realization, the admittance
to myself that I love you
All of the searching through the rubble, embers, and having
hopes has led me to believe that.......
I love everything that I searched to find you, to have you, to
love you
I love you!!!!

"Never doubt the power in which the old possess. We see and hear things that God shows us and tells us. Don't shoot down the significance of insignificant love as my amazing wife tried to warn you. The next time God speaks to you chile, don't be embarrassed to listen. Sometimes you have to contemplate and pray someone into existence. Never doubt the power of our God. Now it's time for me to go dance forever gracefully with my wife. Love Mr. Jamison."

ABOUT THE AUTHOR

Torey has been writing for about 20 years. His writing journey started as a freshman while doing a project in English class. It was then when he figured out what he wanted to do. Torey's burning pen started and has not stopped 15 years later, he enjoys writing about Love, Romance, Sex and really anything that crosses his mind or heart. He also broke into the novel world, writing his first novel "Dr. T Chronicles: Ocular Deception" which can be purchased under the "Order books" tab, along with his poetry book "Love Rescue."

Torey resides in Plano, Tx with the love of his life, Shelba Irving, whom he says, has made his writing 100x better. She inspires him and keeps him going. They have 2 beautiful girls, Londyn and Anaya and they enjoy just making each other happy. Many people want to know what inspires Torey. It's been mentioned that he just loves to know that a woman feels great about herself and loves to see women smiling. Through his writing, he hopes to give women an escape, if only for a moment, he hopes to leave an imprint through his writing to make women feel and know how special they are and they should expect to be treated like the queens that they are.

Torey Irving can be reached by:

Email: passioninkpublishing@gmail.com

Website: www.passioninkpub.com

www.ingramcontent.com/pod-product-compliance
Lightning Source LLC
Chambersburg PA
CBHW050937120626
46552CB00001B/257